RESTORED

Bone Frog Bachelor Series

Book Two

SHARON HAMILTON

ABOUT THE BOOK

Marco and Shannon's hot liquid romance scorches the Florida Gulf Coast

Marco Gambini's Bone Frog Development begins building the Trident Towers project on the Gulf Coast of Florida, managing a diverse team of characters including the two princes, Khalil and Absalom, sons of the Sultan of Bonin... but Rebecca, his vindictive and controlling ex, is doing everything she can to sabotage the project and his relationship with his fiancée Shannon.

Marco also begins building Shannon's dream home nearby. But this former SEAL finds hosting two pampered princelings, who have never in their lives lived without servants and have never done any hard labor, proves more problematic than previously thought.

Shannon finds exciting new challenges, learning about Marco's unique sexual needs, and experimenting with her own triggers and desires as she explores her limits. Their love burns deeper in all areas as they plan a lavish and eccentric wedding at the Pink Palace.

A quick trip to Central Africa to check on the approval and permitting process leads to sudden danger and near-death for part of the team. Shannon learns even more about how her trust in Marco could save them both.

But be warned. There are storm clouds brewing. All is not as it seems. You'll want to continue with Book 3 coming next Spring, *Revenge*.

SHARON HAMILTON'S BOOK LIST

SEAL BROTHERHOOD BOOKS

SEAL BROTHERHOOD SERIES

Accidental SEAL Book 1

Fallen SEAL Legacy Book 2

SEAL Under Covers Book 3

SEAL The Deal Book 4

Cruisin' For A SEAL Book 5

SEAL My Destiny Book 6

SEAL of My Heart Book 7

Fredo's Dream Book 8

SEAL My Love Book 9

SEAL Encounter Prequel to Book 1

SEAL Endeavor Prequel to Book 2

Ultimate SEAL Collection Vol. 1 Books 1-4 /2 Prequels

Ultimate SEAL Collection Vol. 2 Books 5-7

SEAL BROTHERHOOD LEGACY SERIES

Watery Grave Book 1

Honor The Fallen Book 2

Grave Injustice Book 3

BAD BOYS OF SEAL TEAM 3 SERIES

SEAL's Promise Book 1

SEAL My Home Book 2

SEAL's Code Book 3

Big Bad Boys Bundle Books 1-3

BAND OF BACHELORS SERIES

Lucas Book 1

Alex Book 2

Jake Book 3

Jake 2 Book 4

Big Band of Bachelors Bundle

BONE FROG BROTHERHOOD SERIES

New Year's SEAL Dream Book 1

SEALed At The Altar Book 2

SEALed Forever Book 3

SEAL's Rescue Book 4

SEALed Protection Book 5

Bone Frog Brotherhood Superbundle

BONE FROG BACHELOR SERIES

Bone Frog Bachelor Book 0.5

Unleashed Book 1

Restored Book 2

Revenge Book 3

SUNSET SEALS SERIES

SEALed at Sunset Book 1

Second Chance SEAL Book 2

Treasure Island SEAL Book 3

Escape to Sunset Book 4

The House at Sunset Beach Book 5

Second Chance Reunion Book 6

Love's Treasure Book 7

Finding Home Book 8 (releasing summer 2022)
Sunset SEALs Duet #1
Sunset SEALs Duet #2

LOVE VIXEN
Bone Frog Love

SHADOW SEALS
Shadow of the Heart

SILVER SEALS SERIES
SEAL Love's Legacy

SLEEPER SEALS SERIES
Bachelor SEAL

STAND ALONE BOOKS & SERIES
SEAL's Goal: The Beautiful Game
Nashville SEAL: Jameson
True Blue SEALS Zak
Paradise: In Search of Love
Love Me Tender, Love You Hard

NOVELLAS
SEAL You In My Dreams Magnolias and Moonshine

PARANORMALS

GOLDEN VAMPIRES OF TUSCANY SERIES
Honeymoon Bite Book 1

Mortal Bite Book 2

Christmas Bite Book 3

Midnight Bite Book 4

THE GUARDIANS

Heavenly Lover Book 1

Underworld Lover Book 2

Underworld Queen Book 3

Redemption Book 4

FALL FROM GRACE SERIES

Gideon: Heavenly Fall

NOVELLAS

SEAL Of Time Trident Legacy

All of Sharon's books are available on Audible, narrated by the talented J.D. Hart.

CHAPTER 1

I, THE SOON-TO-BE Mrs. Marco Gambini, had a lot to think about this morning as I did my routine run down the sugar-sand beach of Belleair Beach. Marco had left late the night before, taking a flight to D.C. to meet with some senators who could run interference for his Trident Towers project on the Florida Gulf Coast. They were having issues with local building officials concerning their redesign, and he needed powerful allies to help smooth the kinks.

Plans for our wedding in the new year were going well, although most of it was outside my control since we'd accepted the Sultan of Bonin's invitation to host the entire event, including any guests we wished to invite, at his private island in the Indian Ocean. He would house most guests in his Pink Palace and others at various other hotel-like properties on the pink coral beaches. The sultan's wives and servants were preparing everything, and all I had to do was pick out my dress, write my vows, and show up for the party.

Meanwhile, Marco designed a dream home for the two of us to live in on property he'd owned for several years, near his veterans' housing project. I was learning to make decisions: figuring room sizes, placement of windows, overall layout of the house footprint and future gardens surrounding a large pool right on the beach. The house was so overwhelming in size and scope I was having a hard time sleeping. Colors, numbers, building materials, and decorating samples floated around in her brain.

But as complicated as all these decisions and plans were, that wasn't what had me preoccupied. *Worried* wasn't really the right word. How could someone so incredibly lucky worry about a thing, I wondered. Yet something bothered me, and it made no sense.

Marco had asked me to quit my job at TMBC, the TV station in Tampa where I had worked as a part-time weather girl before my recent promotion to reporter. I was rumored to be on the fast track for an anchor position. It was what I'd dreamt of being since I applied at the station—ever since she got my acting and deportment coach after my brief experience acting in a couple of indie films and nearly being cast in a TV series.

And yet, he asked me to give all that up. It wasn't a career like his years in the Navy as an elite SEAL or as

CEO of several multi-billion-dollar companies. I was technically part-time, could be fired at any minute and made very little money. I had to get up incredibly early, which meant getting in a dark run on the beach and shower, driving into work just before sunrise when I'd rather be in bed snuggling with my fiancé—the strongest, most gentle and patient man on the planet with a body twice as hard and sculpted in the flesh as he looked in interviews.

I found myself dreamily longing for my days off when he could show me the passion he felt for me as he extracted that same ardor from me in return. Their all-consuming multi-hour lovemaking sessions made me weak at the knees whenever I thought of them.

But…

I'd acquiesced to moving into the big, beautiful home we were building, even considering letting go of my little beach bungalow when the time came. But quitting my job—that was going to take some special courage.

I wondered why.

And this morning, even though the crisp saltwater sprays, the calls of the sea birds, and the dark purple sky turning pink with dark grey clouds appearing out of nowhere reminded me of all that was good and perfect about my life, I was afraid to cut off the old ties to the sleepy little beach town that helped me heal after the death of my sister—the woman Marco Gambini had been engaged to until her fatal accident. My sister should have been the one to enjoy this abundance and joy, even the excitement and danger that came with Marco and his lifestyle.

I needed to hold something back, something private and all my own, something more precious than my little bungalow. My work gave me a career to fall back on if the unthinkable were to happen—if suddenly Marco were taken from me or left for some reason.

Maybe it was an insurance policy. It wouldn't support the life I was living now, but I could throw myself into it, if I needed to.

I asked myself repeatedly whether I was indeed happy living this life my older sister, Emily, had intended on having with Marco. Or was I playacting? Was it just something I told myself was a dream come true? Was this really a dream I ought to be head over heels about or did I want it because it was something Em would have loved? Again, was I living in Em's place when it came right down to it?

Although I loved Marco more than anyone else in the whole world and knew I'd feel that way forever, the thought of cutting off my past and all my ties to the girl I used to be terrified me. It made me dream about running away, bolting from the idyllic life as a billionaire's fiancée and exchanging it for something common, something I was used to, could trust. I would never be able to return. I didn't want to give up what I'd worked so hard to attain at the station. I'd built it all by myself, too. And I liked my job.

Back and forth, I tossed these ideas as my feet turned down the beach access bridge to Beach Trail Drive, then across an alleyway to Gulf Boulevard, and into the small three-block subdivision of more modest homes. I headed toward the marshes of the dog park and the inlet of Tampa Bay beyond. The gentle tap, tap, tap of my running shoes on the sandy path at the park was in tandem with my breathing, also keeping track with the swishing of my ponytail under my Rays baseball cap. Using my earbuds connected to my trusty old wristband player, I listened as voices sang a sad dirge for a slow king's coronation march. The instruments underneath enhanced the emotions of the singers.

I wound around the outside of the gated doggie play area and heard occasional traffic noises on the wet pavement of Gulf Boulevard and the distinctive rumble of a large diesel truck pulling into the parking lot. The motor stopped, which caused me to stare at it. The windows were blackened, and I could see the glow of a cigarette being lit inside the cab but had no visibility of the driver's face.

Instinct told me to slip on over to the marsh trail

between mangos, sea grapes, and scrub oaks with moss dangling precariously in the light of the full moon like on a Disney ride. Cicadas and other insects chirped and formed their own chorus, creating an almost pulsing sound filled with thousands of tiny reedy voices. I was exploring a back way out that I'd heard about but never seen before, so I kept my running pace.

The truck door slammed.

I felt a spike in my awareness that I might be in some danger, and I silenced my earbuds. My deep thoughts had made me blind to the possibility that perhaps this driver had followed me here to the park, intending on God knew what. I was struck with the ridiculous thought about how quickly my choices were now limited to living or perhaps not living or being harmed. Forget the regret at the TV station, every-thing—the good and the bad—might be taken away in a flash.

I felt vibration through the wooden planks as a heavy man's footsteps shook the boards beneath my feet. I dared not to turn to look for fear he'd seen the terror now resident in my face.

As I rounded a slight curve to the left, I examined my choices. Both sides of the walkway were filled with thick greenery, oversized Elephant Ear plants, man-groves, and wild Bird of Paradise trees going up forty feet or more. But the water was of unknown depth. Between the right side and the left, I couldn't tell which was deeper or which would be more hazardous if I leapt over the railing and attempted to escape through the jungle of foliage.

I chose the right without hesitating. I grabbed the railing and used it to pole vault, swinging my legs up over the wood. Landing mid-calve in the cool water, I winced as the splash was a little too loud. Ripples disrupted the glassy surface of the marsh. The telltale sign revealed something big had landed there: me. I quickly took a step behind a large mangrove and squatted, feeling the coolish water through the seat of my pants, and breathed shallowly. My pulse raced.

A pair of white cranes flew off into the early morning air, their warning cry further revealing my location. But I still waited and hoped the stories were true that crocs didn't like the saltwater marshes and would only invade those areas to feast.

And that could mean...

Suddenly, a flash of light crossed the sky, briefly lighting up the dark grey clouds and the tops of the water-slogged greenery. The crack left my ears pinging, certain that it had landed not far away. I was stranded in a huge marsh of water, with lightning all around me as the second and third flashes and cracks developed, making me jump. Various other birds flew up each time the crack and resulting boom hit the area. I could see the wooden handrail bouncing in the pressure of the early morning storm.

I tried to still myself, but my heart bounced all around in my chest, my shallow breathing making me lightheaded. I was grateful for the commotion, even though it drowned out the footsteps of the approaching man. And when it was at last quiet, as the rain began to trickle down, I heard nothing at all. Just the drizzle—the water washing over everything, as if wiping away whatever had lurked there.

Something grazed past my leg just above my ankle, and I inhaled sharply, about to scream before I remembered the presence of the stranger. So, as I listened for more signs of him, I looked down at my legs in the water, hoping against hope that I wouldn't see a slithering snake or sea worm. It was just black, mucky water. And now I noticed it smelled of old decay and rotting wood. I nearly gagged.

Squinting through the greenery and without making any sound in the water, I attempted to view the path from which I'd just come and found it completely empty.

Stretching my arms out behind me, I carefully rose, felt a large boulder big and solid enough to sit on, and leaned back to make a perch of it. My knees and calves rewarded me with a thank you. My heart rate began to die down. My breathing extended into long, deep takes as I realized, with the feel of daylight approaching sometime in the next hour, I would soon be fully exposed.

Almost as if reassuring me, I heard the diesel engine kick in. The truck shifted gears and then shifted again and sounded like it pulled off onto Gulf Boulevard. Then it was gone.

I waited about a minute longer and then, slowly and without a sound, slid her my shoes over the lumpy rocks and mud in the marsh, reached the walkway, placed her my hands on the path, and hoisted herself myself up to seated position with her legs dangling. As I examined my wet shoes, socks, and ankles, I realized wild, rotting grasses wound around my lower leg, at first looking like tiny snakes. The harmless dead reeds were easily brushed away. The mud was scraped off my shoes and ankles with my forefinger.

And then I stood.

I had two choices, walk along the path through the unknown area of the neighbor's yard somewhere off in the distance based on information that may or may not be accurate or go back the way I came where I could call someone—except that I hadn't brought my cell because Marco was unreachable, still enroute, and probably sleeping in the back of a black limo.

But going back the same way I'd arrived seemed

safest, so I started home with a brisk walk, gradually advancing it into a jog. My shoes shed bubbles of grey water and squeaked as if I was running on baby mice.

Except this time, I wasn't thinking about the sadness of giving up my job. I was grateful no truck lingered in the empty parking lot, nor was there a truck along Gulf Boulevard, the hundred steps until I made it to the Beach Access trail and Beach Trail Drive, or to my own front door.

Once inside, I locked and deadbolted the ten-light glass-paned door, vowing to replace it with something more difficult to breach as soon as I could arrange it.

I'd gotten so used to the feel of Marco beside me nearly twenty-four seven, I'd allowed my mind to wander into the ridiculous depths, nitpicking and finding fault with something that had come to me like a miracle—a Navy Blue dream of a man who loved me so hard I might not have to worry about anything ever again.

Except someone, somewhere might be wanting to take all that away from me. I wouldn't make that mistake again. This could all be taken away just like that flash of lightning, just like what had befallen my sister, dying in the car accident along with her friends from school. How quickly things could change if I didn't protect this gift of life.

I vowed never to complain about any of my feckless

reasoning about all the choices I was making. I would embrace those choices so hard they could never be torn even from my cold, lifeless fingers at the very end. I'd hang on and never, ever give up hope or take for granted my perfect life.

This isn't for you, Em. It's for me.

CHAPTER 2

I FELT SHANNON'S warm body purring next to me, spiking my libido and turning on all my senses. Even my fingertips craved the touch of her flesh as I reached over to gently crawl up the inside of her thigh—caressing the perfectly baby smooth of her body—as her hand gripped my wrist. She rolled over on her back, bent her knees, and pressed my palm and those wandering fingers against her sex, moaning as she helped me violate her.

"Tell me how it feels," I whispered. I kissed the side of her neck and squeezed her nether lips, causing her to arch up and present those perfectly formed breasts as my gift. "Give them to me, Shannon," I begged hoarsely.

She did as she was told, as she always did when I commanded she do something in bed. It wasn't me being overbearing; it was me showing her how much I needed the friction of my flesh against her soft pink parts, her long smooth parts, and the hairless parts of her belly, her rear, her forearms, and those long silky legs.

Her eyes were open as she arched farther. She placed her warm and slightly sweaty chest against mine, wrapping one leg up and over my hip.

She looked straight at me as I inserted my thumb again into her channel.

"Give it to me, Marco." She smiled and let her little pink tongue dart around her lips. I sighed at the perfect view of my lover in full arousal, longing for the salty taste of her sweet juices.

I inserted my thumb again, playing with her, mocking her erotic impatience. She rubbed my fingers over her clit and forced my thumb and forefinger to squeeze the tiny nub, which made her squeal, throw her head to the side, and arch her pelvis up to rub against my belly button. Then she climbed over my hip and rubbed herself back and forth over my protruding hip bone.

With her arms pressed together, her blonde hair all a mess like I liked it, her breasts protruding seductively while she ground away on me, she whispered, "Make me come, Marco. I want you inside me."

I flipped her quickly on her back and impaled her, throwing her knee up over my shoulder as I rammed my cock deep, moaning with her. Her wet channel vibrated all around me and drew me in even deeper.

"Oh my God!"

"Yes?" My half smile was intended as a joke, but she was serious.

"You can't ever leave me. I want to walk around all day with you inside me. I want to stay in bed until the sun comes up tomorrow, and I still want you to be fucking me, making me sore, taking me any way you want while I still want more. Make me a rag doll, Marcos. I want to be exhausted, used, pleasured, and lit on fire."

"No problem, baby. Hang on so we can fly together. Give me just—"

And then I began to spill, which nearly set me in tears because I'd wanted to fuck her senseless, and now that dream was gone.

"I like it when you come fast. You know I do," she whispered.

And indeed, I did. She loved making me lose control. She loved showing me that there was no way in Holy Hell that I could ever resist her or wouldn't want to ravish her to oblivion. I'd fuck her while she laughed at my expense because I loved seeing her face as I did it. For, no matter how hard I tried to exert control, she was my better. She was the spark that lit me on fire every time. I would never get enough.

And in five minutes, with enough breathing exercises and mental meditation, I'd be bigger and harder again, ever bigger and harder than the first time. And then I'd love that look on her face as I pierced her veil and surprised her.

In the shower, I told her about my trip. Yes, I'd gotten the support I was looking for from Senator Campbell and two of his colleagues. I was guaranteed a quick review of the final plan by the Veterans Housing Board without a senate hearing, which would be a huge waste of time and cause months of delay. I was promised that they would intercede, if necessary, with county and city building officials who might make problems for me or who owed an allegiance to my ex, who had originally sent in her design that I fixed.

She was soaping off my back when she brought up the subject of her safety when I was gone.

"Something happen?"

She rubbed my back with the lavender gel she used on her body, which would not make my skin as smooth and smell as nice as hers, but I was okay with it. And then she rubbed more gel, her fingers barely smoothing over my back. Her non-verbal communication told me something was brewing, and I wouldn't like it. She was unhappy she'd made me aware of it too.

"No, silly. But I was just thinking, you know how I take those morning runs along the beach? I was wondering if perhaps I should get a permit to carry a gun. Or carry mace or something. Cat's claws, you know, for defense."

I turned, and her eyes were downturned, avoiding mine.

"What is it, Shannon?"

"I said it's nothing. My imagination, I guess. This time when you went away, I just got jumpy. I started seeing things or imagining—wondering how I would defend myself if someone came up behind me or jumped from the bushes. I've had so much on my mind with the summer plans and the wedding—"

"Which you don't have to do anything for. You are remembering that, right?"

"Yes. Yes. But there is the guest list, gathering everyone's addresses, picking out my dress, and writing our vows... unless you're going to use something you've found in a Navy manual somewhere."

That's when she finally looked up at me, her long lashes dripping with wet goodness, the innocence of her face a sweet mask over the powerful woman I knew lived inside. Her tempting little comment, needling me, making fun of my uniform code of conduct even as she reveled in breaking me down.

I pressed her against the tile of her little shower, suddenly grateful for the tight spot. "Tell me that again, but look at me this time," I whispered, glancing my hungry lips across hers as if I was breathing life into her soul.

When she smiled, hesitating to answer me back, I placed my hands under her jaw, tilted her head back, and kissed her long and hard. I wanted her wet and slippery. When we parted, her eyes were filled with tears.

"You overwhelm me, Marco," she said before I could ask. "Sometimes, I fear not having you." She looked at my biceps, palming my upper arm from shoulder to elbow joint and back again. The smooth and hairless mound of her sex slipped by my thigh, and its proximity to the root of my soul made my pecker vibrate.

"The same goes for me, sweetheart. I must go to sleep with cold towels wrapped around my waist. I run into walls and wake up with the biggest boner—even bigger than when I was in my twenties. I am a distracted, mess of a man who's without his mate—"

"The solution is easy, then. We'll never be apart. I mean it, Marco."

"Is that healthy?"

"You mean you couldn't carry on your business with your fat dick inside me?"

"Shannon, that's not nice…"

"I have a serious craving."

"Then let's fix it right now."

I whipped her around, bent her over, went to my

knees. Before she could object, I had my tongue deep inside her cave, the water crashing down upon us both. I nibbled and sucked, ran her delicate lips through my canines, and accessorized her moans with some of my own. I sucked her bud by spreading her cheeks wide, searching for her most intimate bright pink pretty parts. I inserted my tongue, rolling it in and out, and added a thumb. Then I got to my feet and slid my cock deep inside her, one hand on her belly to hold her tight against me, the other keeping her bent over for optimum penetration.

With my thighs, I made a seat for her while she wrapped her lower legs and ankles around mine and forced herself against me, pushing against the tiled wall with her palms. The crescendo built, the water was going cold, and it mattered not one bit as she squealed, inhaled, then shattered all over me. I pumped furiously. She resisted and then began to shake, demanding, clutching around to my buttocks with one hand, at last holding firm against me until they both felt the delicious spurt of my seed.

It had begun to occur to me during these especially deep penetrations that we'd stopped using protection. I didn't think it was possible that I couldn't fill her belly with a thousand babies. And I'd love them all.

Her face was pressed against the now-cold tile as she started to giggle, like she'd been drinking. I cupped cold water and washed her sex with careful fingers.

"It's not going to work," she said.

"What?"

"I can't be fixed." She turned, her face flushed and rosy, red lips mesmerizing me. My heart hung on her every word, and that's exactly how attentive I intended to be.

"I don't want you to be fixed. I want you afflicted, craving me, so I know what you mean, Shannon. I can't be fixed either. I never want this to change."

"Then let's try not to be separated."

Oh, this again.

I was sure something had happened. I turned off the cold water, grabbed a white fluffy towel, wrapped it around her, and then carried her to the bedroom without allowing her to dry her hair. I dropped her onto the tussled sheets and pulled them up to her chin, unwrapping them from her legs. I sat, peering over her, still dripping wet, wanting to make her tell me what had happened.

"You brought up the safety issue, Shannon. Not me. If it will make you feel more secure, I'll have you apply for the CCW permit and enroll you in the course, and I'll weapons train you. We'll pick out your personal sidearm together. I'll make suggestions and you tell me what feels the most comfortable."

She smiled. "Thank you, Marco. That would mean

a lot."

"So what brought all this on, Shannon?" I asked, hoping the sugar of her possible new weapon and training would sufficiently assuage her from keeping her barrier up.

She gulped air then began her story—a story I wasn't looking forward to hearing, but one I must hear, nonetheless.

"Two days ago, the day you left for D.C., I was imagining things like crazy. A big truck rumbled suddenly into the dog park where I was finishing up and parked. I saw the flare of a lighter behind the tint, but the windows were too dark for me to see the person. And when I came back and looked around, there was no evidence of the truck anywhere. I think it was just my mind playing tricks on me. Maybe with a conceal permit I'd not have those kinds of disturbing thoughts."

I was more concerned than I let on. "But think, Shannon. Was there a truck following you or not?"

"I thought so. But whoever it was drove off before I could see them."

"I meant, did he follow you along Gulf Boulevard or just when you got to the dog park?"

She shrugged. "I don't know the answer to that."

"So what made you *think* he was following you?"

"Because I hadn't been paying attention. I realized

when I heard and then saw him that he could have been following me earlier, but I never noticed it until the park. I'm sorry, Marco, but it's the truth."

I had to acknowledge her courage to admit her distraction. Anger boiled up inside my belly, but I knew it would completely end the conversation, or worse, end it with an argument. "What happened next?"

Her voice was quiet, timid like a little girl's at first. Then she spoke up, seeing me lean over and bend an ear.

"I thought I heard his footsteps on the wooden planks of the path."

Fucking pervert! Now I wasn't regretting the facts. I craved them so I could skin this moron alive and drag his carcass behind my Hummer all up and down the Florida coastline as a lesson to anyone else who would mess with my woman.

I did two silent box breathings and then spoke to her calmly. "So, Shannon, he *was* following you then, wasn't he?" I was irritated with Shannon's lack of specificity. She said she didn't see his face but that he smoked. The windows in the truck had all been blackened, a common occurrence in Florida. "Did anyone else see him?"

"I don't think so. This was like five-thirty in the morning, before sunrise."

"And you were off the beach and the beach trail."

"Yes."

"Why the hell would you go over to the dog park? There aren't lights there. No one should be there at that time of the day. It's asking for trouble, Shannon."

"I have no clue, Marco. It was just the place that came up next. As I already stated, I was thinking about the wedding, and the—the other stuff we talked about. I was going to come right home afterwards, before the sun rose, and get to the station near sunrise. That's always what I do."

"What other stuff?"

"It's not important now."

"Fuck's sake, it is." I saw her eyes flash wide. "Sorry. I want to know everything you were thinking and why."

"That's another conversation, Marco. And yes, we'll have it. But it doesn't have anything to do with the situation. It would be off track to go there."

She was hiding something, and I didn't like it. But I'd already gotten way more out of her than I'd expected. I breathed another couple of reps and felt my blood pressure calm, but my heart still pounded, my fists needing to punch and fight.

"Promise me you'll change your routine. No more running before sunrise." I knew she would be lying if she said yes.

"That's why I wanted to talk to you about personal

carry or mace or something for protection."

"But why become someone's bait in the first place? Why tempt someone who might be looking for an opportunity thrill. Evil does exist, Shannon. That's just not smart."

She nodded, and because she was lying down, I could see the tears spill over her cheekbones into the pillow. I gently spread them over her beautiful face, sending the liquid into her hair with my thumbs, bent down, and kissed her.

"You are the most valuable thing in my life, Shannon. But I don't own you. That means you must make the kinds of choices that keep you safe, not do stupid things." I gripped her shoulders as she objected to my description.

"Remember that you prove by your actions whether or not you want to spend the rest of your life with me. You do what you do best. And trust me to do what I do. I promise to keep you safe, but you must promise to always use your head. That means when you're busy, you always have eyes at the back of your head, your ears must hear things you didn't before hear as patterns, things that we've seen and heard on the Teams. You must notice how people look at you and when they don't. You always check for multiple ways to get out of a situation, whether it's a meadow, a street, or a room. You have to determine what you have to break, who you have to punch or kick, and always understand that, if you're prepared, you will have the greatest advantage a woman can have."

"What's that?"

"They will underestimate you. You be prepared to deliver them a message they either will never forget or they'll never recover from. You do it without hesitation. You feel good when you do it. You use everything at your disposal, and you win."

CHAPTER 3

MY CONSTRUCTION CREW was delighted with the news that Senator Campbell and his committee were going to help troubleshoot some of the roadblocks we'd been having with the Pinellas County Planning Department concerning the Trident Towers. We went over the improved, final plans—or at least we hoped it would be the final version.

I explained to the group that I'd decided to scale back the size of the fitness center and instead open a PT office, especially for the permanently disabled veterans who were going to constantly need PT work with competent therapists in order to progress in their fitness and health goals. Many of these vets would not have the benefits to cover all the expenses of prosthetic and orthotic work, so the corporation was going to hire a staff orthotist at no charge to the residents. In this way, the gym and ancillary offices would serve as an in-home outpatient clinic for chronic bone and joint injuries, also enabling the vets to take training while remaining in their homes.

I could see that Shannon was in awe how much I cared about my former teammates and other servicemen and women who had sacrificed so much and received so little. She completely understood the community would help heal itself with the concept that we were all still on the same team, and always would be.

"Our ethos is, 'No man or woman left behind,'" I explained at the meeting. "I hope that this will be a model for future vet centers. I wish I had the money to build a hundred of them, and even that wouldn't be enough. These are not throwaway men and women. They are those who answered their highest calling—to serve their country. They serve regardless of religion or race, although the hours are long and dangerous and the pay not commensurate to what they gave up. These men and women are our heroes."

Every time I talked about the project, Shannon saw how straight I stood, how my chest expanded, and how tall I had become. Even with all the problems we'd encountered, my zeal and passion for it only increased.

"Can I ask you a question, Boss?" Rhea, now my newly titled Vice President and Construction Manager at Bone Frog Development, asked me. I'd lured the former president of an all-female construction crew in the Gulf Coast away with my grand ideas and ability to see them through.

"Shoot. What do you need to know?" I replied.

"Just where did you get the idea for this project? I mean, is this a charity, or are we going to make money here?"

"We're going to do both, to answer your second question first. I can't afford to do this as a charity, and I don't dare give it to some non-profit or government agency who will drain the cash as well as the inspiration for it. We're not managing people here. We're transforming people's lives. Veterans' lives."

"But she wants to know why," reminded Dax, Rhea's life partner and second in charge.

"Because it's my calling. Because I'm the one who can get it done. And by done, I don't mean 'check the boxes.' I mean, do it right. Create something that no one else has done before. I'm hoping that if people see what's possible—because people have no imagination for things—once they see it can be done, they'll help organize and back others. I want this idea to catch fire and expand beyond what I could ever do with my companies alone. Think of it as a pilot for a new series."

Watching Shannon study the faces of the group of Bone Frog Development employees, I could tell she was struck with the realization that I had created the most coveted and rare emotion possible: awe. Every face reflected their complete amazement at what had been proposed. Not one person had crossed arms, slouched shoulders, or a skeptical expression. I'd mesmerized the room into silence.

Admitting it to myself, I chuckled. "Well, don't everyone speak at once. You must have bigger questions than that." I shrugged, and in unison, the group politely laughed.

"Now here's where some of my concerns lie," I began again. "Part of this plan incorporates my mission to train the Sultan of Bonin's two sons in managing a large project like this, as a precursor to their African project, which we are helping them run."

Several people shifted uneasily in their chairs.

"Now, I don't know if I can ever whip them into shape. They've spent years being coddled, almost treated as the sultan's pets. And I don't want a word of this to get outside this room, either. Grounds for immediate termination, understood?"

The group followed my playful attitude, some smiling and shaking their heads while others only shaking their heads, "no". But everyone agreed to my rules.

"They are to be treated with respect. They are students of mine. Not my sons, not pampered princelings, they'll be normal twenty-year-old boys learning how to run a business. Their idea of buying and selling is using a credit card to get anything they wanted in life. But they've both done very well in school, have college degrees, and want to learn. This isn't being forced on them by anyone but me."

Again, the room erupted into chuckles and smiles.

"If they treat you without respect, you come straight to me. And yes, you can tell them they did so. Don't be afraid of them. They can't get you fired. Is that understood?"

Again, the team nodded agreement and mumbled to themselves.

"When do they start?" someone asked.

"They'll be here in two days. I'm waiting confirmation on their timing this afternoon." I took two long steps across the front of the room. "Here's another thing, assume they don't know anything. You show them everything you do. Pretend they are your re-placements—and *once again!*—they are not your replacements but pretend that they are. You train them with everything you do. I'm going to hope that some of it sticks."

Rhea chuckled loudest. "Oh boy, it's going to be a long hot summer, Boss. I sure do hope you know what you're doing."

"You're allowed to swear, Rhea. This is our culture here, our country. They won't like it, so keep it at a minimum, if you can. Dax, you help her with that."

"Roger that, Boss Man!" Dax said, jumping to her feet. "I'll need help washing her mouth out with soap, but I'm game to try."

"Let's hope it doesn't come to that. Now. For your homework. I want you to give me a full assessment of where you feel the project's biggest problems are, in your opinion. What is going to be the most difficult hurdle to get over or take the longest to accomplish. I want these reports on my desk tomorrow morning. Nothing is more important today. This also means that if you think I need to hire another key person or you've observed someone on our team can't handle the workload without additional help, you state that. I want to eliminate as many obstacles and issues as possible. I want to train to be prepared for the unexpected."

"So, Top Dog, we get to make suggestions about you, too?" Forest Davis asked. Forest was an expert drone developer and explosives expert. He also knew everything there was to know about poisons and knives, as well as customizing some of their firepower for missions in hostile locations. He had been embarrassed to tell the team that he'd posed for the cover of a romance novel. Shannon had thought that was pretty cool, but he got a lot of ribbing for it.

"Absolutely, you can give me some of your black sarcasm. Go ahead and see how far you can get kicking my butt. But be damned sure, I'll listen," I answered. "I might veto it, but I promise you I'll listen."

Everyone laughed at that one.

"Well, all right then. Here's one for you. You need to give this little lady here some work. I mean, I can guess you guys work pretty hard at home, if you know what I mean."

Everyone chuckled. Shannon blushed, and I adopted a scowl.

"Watch it, Forest…"

"No worries, my man. I was just thinking she looks good here, and I'd like to see her give us some good publicity, maybe sweet talk her way into an interview about what we're doing and drum up some community support, like she did when Rebecca tried to highjack this little opera."

Most everyone agreed. I could see Shannon was delighted.

"Marco, I could write a series of press releases, since I know the look and feel of them, how to do them. I could perhaps get you some interviews with other stations outside Tampa, so it wouldn't interfere with my bosses here. Station affiliates. It would expand our brand and perhaps cull more support."

"I like that, Shannon," I said, giving her a wink. I swung my head over to focus on Forest. "You're way smarter than I sometimes give you for, Forest.

Thanks!"

"I love to be underestimated."

Nigel, who was from Edinburgh, suggested they could even get an interview through his sister's connections there. "She'd love to interview you lot. Always pestering me about the famous Marco Gambini and what he's up to," he said, with the brogue Shannon loved.

Nigel stuttered a bit and added, "And of course, the mysterious woman who bagged that famous playboy. Well, Shannon, she'd love to interview you too!"

I saw Shannon blushing for the second time today.

"We'll set that up, Nigel, thanks."

"Oh, I think it would be so romantic to do a piece about the new house you're building, don't you?" Karin Atkin asked Shannon. "We could put her up in one of Marco's properties and give her the tour. I'll bet she'd consider it an experience of a lifetime!"

"She would at that, dearie," Nigel agreed. "Her nickers would be in a bunch for weeks afterward. I keep telling her about this place. She might never go home, and me mum would have my tail for that. But it happens." He shrugged while the team laughed.

"I'll get you my list of things I'd need and personnel, Marco, by the morning," Shannon smiled up at me, which caused my bushy greying eyebrows to raise.

"You do that, my love, and you'll get a gold star," I

whispered and then winked again, while running my finger along Shannon's spine, sending a pleasurable zing of electricity from the base of Shannon's neck to her toes.

The meeting was adjourned. Dax and Rhea came up to speak to me in private, so Shannon stepped discretely away.

"Hey, Shannon, don't go slinking off. You can hear this too," barked Rhea.

"What gives? Hope this isn't a resignation, because…"

"Relax, Boss," Rhea said as she spread her hands to the sides and let her shoulders raise. "We have a delicate matter to discuss. And, well," she looked at Dax, "we want your blessing."

"What the hell have you two cooked up?" I sounded angry, but I was playing with them.

"Dax and I want to get married. All legal-like. You've been very good to us. We've made good money, and we're ready to buy a house, and, well, we just wanted to be legit." Rhea searched Shannon's face as well as mine.

"You already are legit," I said to them. "You love each other, and everyone knows it. You don't have to get married to…"

"Then why are you doing it, Marco?" asked Dax.

I stepped back, clearly blindsided by the question. I

examined my hands and then looked up. "Touché, Dax. You're right." And then to Shannon, I instructed, "Cancel the wedding. We don't need any paperwork or wedding to show the world we love each other."

Shannon froze in place but then saw the twinkle in my eye.

"You know, Boss, you're a fuckin' asshole," shouted Rhea so loud some of the other team turned around to watch. But then she grabbed me and gave me a hug. "I'm not taking no for an answer. We want you to be the one to give Dax away. And I'd like to walk down the aisle with the lovely Shannon!"

"But that's reserved for your dad," Shannon objected, but I could tell, inside she was dancing.

"Fuck that bastard. That sonofabitch doesn't deserve that honor. He's completely out of my rolodex. But I have some nieces and a few nephews who might come, and we'd like to make it a simple, elegant party. Nothing fancy. And could we use the Towers building site? Just make it a beach party. Invite some of the would-be owners and tenants?"

"Sounds like a lovely idea, Rhea. I'd be honored." I had extricated myself from Rhea's strong body slam and bowed to her respectfully as if she were Queen for a Day. Dax stood to the side, her hands clasped, tears running down her face.

"Awesome!" Rhea hugged her partner. "We're doing this, Dax. I told you he'd be good about it."

I added one more condition.

"But let's get the final permits, okay? I don't want to count our chickens before they roost. I sure as hell wouldn't want you to be disappointed to have to cancel your big day just based on some bureaucrat's say so. We need to remove that hurdle first. Then it's all out, okay?"

CHAPTER 4

I TOLD SHANNON I had plans for us for dinner.

"Oh really? Where to?"

"You'll see. Something special."

"I should go home and change. Is it fancy, a fancy restaurant?"

I loved surprising her. "*Very* fancy. But you're dressed fine."

Shannon looked over the sundress and sandals she was wearing and frowned. "I wish I could wash my hair and put on clean undies. I've been sweating all day."

"It makes no difference to me."

"Well, it might make some difference to the other guests. I smell like a road crew member."

I pulled her to me. "Stop it, Shannon. I get some say here. And I say you're perfect. Besides," I checked my watch, "we don't have a lot of time left."

"What time is the reservation?"

I checked my watch again. "7:21."

Shannon wrested free. "Stop making fun of this, Marco. No one makes a reservation for 7:21. Come on. Quit pulling my leg."

"I do. I do a lot of things other people don't. Just humor me, go freshen up in the bathroom if you want, but we need to be outta here in like ten."

"It's going to take us that long to get there? Tell me we're not flying or something."

"No, but that gives me a good idea for next time." I placed my hands on her shoulders, turned her around, and demanded, "March!" directing her to the ladies' room, which was stocked with towels and deodorants. I knew Shannon stored a couple of lipsticks and some perfume in the cabinet for occasions as this.

While she was occupied, I chose a tube from my office and slipped it into the back of my Hummer. Folded next to it were three large Turkish muslin beach towels. Shannon stepped out, and we were on our way.

"At least tell me where."

"You'll see."

She leaned back into the seat, resigned that her inquiries would yield the same result as the previous ones: nothing.

"I got you registered for Wyatt's permit class. And if you're interested, his daughter does a women's self-defense class. Just let me know, and I'll get you registered for that one too."

"Thanks, Marco. You know this guy, Wyatt?"

"Very well. Marine sharpshooter, even tried out for the Olympics. He was one of their best instructors and, later, joined the Tampa police force where he's taught classes nearly his whole career. Now he's retired, so it's his full-time gig. Wyatt's a smart fellow who teaches you all the things you need to know and all the things you don't know to ask. You'll have a healthy respect for firearms when you're done."

"So next is picking out one. Is that it?"

"Yup, I was thinking we could go look tomorrow if we get done in time. Your classes don't start for three weeks, plenty of time to get your ammunition if it's not in stock. We'll want to get you something that won't be too difficult to arm or expensive, like a 9mm. Some sidearms are great, but the rounds are scarce or overly popular right now."

I turned down Gulf Boulevard, passing the dog park where Shannon had the encounter with the man in the pickup. I noticed that she searched the parking lot.

"Does it still scare you?" I asked.

"Not really. Like you said, it wasn't a very good idea. I'm not going there in the dark and by myself again."

"Do you think you could recognize the truck if you saw it again?"

She shook her head. "Maybe the sound, but then, diesel trucks always sound the same. It had a deep, heavy idle."

"Did you see the grill? Could you tell if it was a Chevy or Ford? Or was it something like this?"

"Not a Hummer. I would have recognized the shape. Even the pickups are different. No, it was a big heavy-duty truck with big tires. And I think it was a four-door model. But that's it."

I turned down one of the avenues to Beach Trail Drive.

"Where are you going? Are we…?"

"Yup. Going to the lot."

"For dinner?"

"I hope so. I paid a boatload for it. We'll see."

Beach Trail ended, and then a dirt road wound around the sand dunes, at last coming through the green foliage to the flat graded plateau prepared for their new home on the five private acres.

I scanned the horizon, now turning purple and orange with golden clouds crossing the horizon and slowly changing shape. In the center of the leveled pad was a table and two benches. The table had a white tablecloth on it, adorned with a bouquet of red roses and a silver champagne bucket with a bottle chilling inside. Surrounding the table was a circle of hurricane lamps, lighted, which showed us the way. I was pleased to notice the red cube food transport box, keeping my special order both warm and chilled.

"This is just beautiful," Shannon gasped as I turned off the engine and we looked at the display in front of us. "How did you do this?"

"Well, obviously, I didn't do this. I hired someone else to do it, because I was with you, right?"

"Oh, Marco, you amaze me how you think of these things."

"Good. Mission accomplished then. Let's get out before it gets cold."

One thing that I loved about the Gulf area was that, even near sunset, the air was still warm, and even if there was a breeze, it was a warm one. Waves crashing in the background infused excitement and unpredictability.

I opened the door for Shannon and led her to the table. Then I went back and brought the blankets and the tube, placing them beside the table. Shannon stood facing the dying sun, her hair blowing in ringlets behind her. She turned.

"I don't think I'll ever tire of this view. I love it from my little place, but from here, with all the privacy around us, it's spectacular."

I uncorked the champagne and brought her a glass. We touched, kissed, then sipped the light pink liquid.

"To happily ever afters. To new beginnings. To imagining and then creating miracles. That's our life now, Shannon. This is what every day will be like from now on."

Her face was lined with tears. She sipped her champagne and leaned into me. "I think this is going to be my best day. We used to play that game when I was little."

"I remember Em telling me that."

"Best company. Best sunset. Best dream come true. Best everything."

"Yes. I'm marrying the girl of my dreams. I will forever be grateful for Em bringing us together. I hope that's something you can embrace."

"I'm getting there," she said.

I pulled my arm around her waist. "Are you hungry?"

"Starved."

I led the way back to the table in the middle of the circle of fire. Pulling out the red insulated box, I unzipped the top layer and placed a chilled platter with a dozen oysters swimming in lemon slices. I handed one shell to her and took one for myself.

"Lemon?" I asked as I held a slice over her oyster.

"Of course."

Having properly garnished the half shells, we both slurped them down. Shannon took another sip of champagne and then reached for another.

The tabletop was still lighted with the lamps all around them. Next on the menu was lobster bisque. The main course was a perfectly poached salmon, still warm, with fresh buttered green beans, and a long grain rice pilaf with pine nuts. Two delicate green salads with a lemony dressing were individually chilled and wrapped as an accompaniment.

For dessert, we had chocolate mousse garnished with golden raspberries.

I was pleased with the presentation and made a note to ask the team to use this caterer again for any of our special events coming up.

I picked up a hurricane lamp and one of the blankets and the tube. "Shall we sit in the living room?"

"Where is it?"

"Here, see for yourself. See if you can tell me where it is." I held the tube to her, and she stretched out the house plans in front of me. With the aid of the lamp, she walked several paces and then pointed to an area. I spread the blanket there and invited her to sit down.

"You approve? You like the living room here?"

"I'd like to study the plans better, but yes, it matches what we talked about. I wanted the living room to be open to the coastline, to watch the sunsets. This is perfect!"

We sat side by side, arms wrapped around each other, continuing to watch the sky turn darker and darker, and then the stars began to come out. Remnants of huge puffy clouds still glowed pink in the afterglow of the sunset against the new night sky.

"Ready for more?"

"Absolutely."

I stood, helped her up, then took the lamp and pointed to the plans. "How about the master bedroom now? We'll have to pretend we're on the second floor."

"So it's back here, because there's a deck off the master suite, which is over the living room. I think the bedroom would start here." She pointed back about twenty feet.

"And where would be the bed?" I asked.

"I'd say against the back wall, so it would have a perfect view of the ocean in the morning and the sunset at night."

"Where?" I asked again.

"Right here." She pointed to one spot, and I lay the blanket down then placed two hurricane lamps on either side. I added another blanket to the corner and then invited her to sit.

"How's the bed?" I asked.

"A little firm, but nice." She linked fingers with mine and leaned into me, placing a kiss on my mouth that lingered. "I can still taste the oysters and the lemon."

"And I think I tasted a little bit of mousse as well."

"Yes."

"Shall we try out the bed?" I asked.

"You mean?"

"Of course. I want to remember this evening for the rest of my life."

"So do I. I see you've brought another blanket."

"So when you're naked you won't be cold. I want to see you naked on my new bed, Shannon. I want to make love to you in our new bedroom. I want to start the memories before the house is built. What do you think of my plan?"

"I think,"—she crawled over my lap and began pulling her dress over the top of her head—"if you don't get me out of these clothes, I'm going to burn up."

I knew I'd never forget this night nor the way she needed me under the twinkling stars, and as she shattered beneath me, I whispered, "I love you more every day, Shannon. You bring the magic. You're the talisman. You're the one who's saved me—you've saved us both."

CHAPTER 5

I WAS TROUBLED again as I drove to the station in Tampa. Marco had never asked me, but I still hadn't done what I'd promised him I'd do, and that was to quit. Even with the suggestion of my helping the team out with interviews and promo features like engaging other stations, producing podcasts, reaching out to my friends in the industry, all of which I'd mentioned in my report on Marco's desk, he didn't ask me about it.

I knew he'd eventually find out. All the mention of my PR work didn't trigger in him a second opinion that maybe I should hold off quitting until sometime in the future. No, on the contrary, he made notations about what he wanted me to do in the upcoming weeks and even mentioned I would be spending more time with him in this process, which of course thrilled me. But it still left me that black hole. I had to face the fact that he was expecting me to quit. I'd given him my word, and that meant I needed to either do it or come clean about my avoidance and have a damned good reason why.

I hated all these back-and-forth things bouncing around my brain. I wished I had the focus and deliberative skills Marco had. "Life would be so much easier," I whispered to myself while driving across the Causeway that led from the beach communities on the island and the mainland of Florida—Tampa my destination.

My lesson of the other morning still gurgled in my stomach, with how close I might have been to a negative situation. My attempts to downplay it were a no-go with Mr. Super-mind-reader-and-all-round-God-Marco. He could see through my little ruse as if I wrote it on six-foot posters in front of him.

He told me it was because of his training, his practice. It had been drilled into him. He practiced mind control, box breathing, meditating every morning (when I didn't interrupt him) and every night. He told me he was gaining back the strength he had when he was in his peak.

"You are at your peak, Marco. Just look at you," I'd said when he explained this to me.

"Nope. Not even close. My awareness isn't what it used to be. There's a big difference too. You must feel the danger, and trust me, it's all around you all the time. There's always evil. We want to think everything is good and happy, fairies and such. But those are brief glimpses of a world that could be but isn't for very long. We grab it and enjoy it when we can. Other times, we embrace the suck. We adapt, train for the unexpected, so we aren't caught off guard with no solutions."

And that's exactly what had happened the other morning.

I was so unlike him in so many ways, stubborn just like Em, but neither of us ever dwelled in a place of expecting evil and danger. We both had lived in a bubble, that HEA bubble where if the two of us obeyed the rules, were good to people, our lives would turn out to be picture perfect.

But Em's accident and death was a perfect example of an HEA gone horribly wrong. And that day at her funeral, when Marco bent down and handed me that flower from Em's grave, looking right into my 12-year-old eyes, I knew he would forever be my warrior, my savior, and the man I was destined to be with. If that meant learning how to shoot a gun, box breathing, meditating, and mind control, so be it. I'd do whatever it took, give up whatever I had to, to be with this man.

Even my job at the station.

I pulled into the parking lot, already flooded with vehicles. It was going to be another Florida scorcher, something I still had difficulty adjusting to. The island was usually a bit cooler, with the breezes we got there sometimes, like a gentle mother whispering that the oppressive heat wouldn't last long. In California, I could leave my windows open at night and the whole house would be cool by early morning. But many summer days in Florida, the temperature needle, even in a rainstorm or hurricane, sometimes never moved.

Though I heard birds barking back and forth at each other from the forty-foot palm trees lining the station entrance, the pavement I walked across seemed to hiss.

Once inside the lobby, which had recently installed a waterfall feature that gave the main floor a chlorine odor, I passed security, nodding to the two female guards manning the reception desk. I took the elevator to the fifth floor, where the programming and accounting offices were located, and inquired about setting an appointment with Jared Newsome. They promised some time with him after my broadcast. I knew he wouldn't arrive until well after seven, just as I was about to go on the air. Today, they were giving me a feature to read, hooking up with a local reporter giving updates on the red tide affecting sea life on the island, as well as the all-important tourist trade.

I took the elevator up a floor and came to the production level where the studio was located. I walked toward the Green Room, stopping by Sandy's makeup station to have my face painted. A new script had been left there on the counter for me to review before I went live.

"OK, I gonna make you look real pretty so you can tell that story about all those poor dead fish."

"Yes." I sighed. "You've been reading my mail?"

"Well, God yes. Gotta have some perks of working here. Those pictures are disgusting. I'm gonna give your fans something pretty to look at."

Sandy began spraying my hair with dry shampoo and doing a quick curl with the iron.

"Bear in mind there are going to be live shots from the scene. We only use these when the feed doesn't work. You do know that."

"Like I said, those poor dead fish. Nobody cares about the fish lying on the beach stinking up things. It gives the little one's nightmares, not very romantic for couples strolling hand in hand by moonlight."

"I agree with you there," I added.

"And where's Greenpeace? But no, you kill a couple of whales or a dolphin or if a Croc takes a toddler and, OMG, you'd think the world came to an end. It's like those salamanders in California. Tiger something. My sister said they practically shut down all housing developments in Bakersfield over those little things nobody would ever see. Must look at them with special lights at night. They threw themselves at police cars and chained themselves in front of the EPA in Sacramento, yet these fishes?" She shrugged. "Nobody cares. They just want them outta here."

"Good summer job for some."

"Are you kidding? You know the guy who picks up dog poop in all the Pinellas County dog parks makes about sixty grand a year! Can you believe that?"

"What are you going to do? Can't have that stuff everywhere."

"They want dogs to be able to poop all over places, let fish die on the beaches because someone kills all the sea grass by dumping phosphates into the gulf, but oh boy, you kill those salamanders, and you lose your right to have a house. I think this place is hella mixed up."

"You know, Sandy, one day I'm going to interview you, and then you can tell them what's truth. *Life of Sandy* and all your past adventures."

"Oh God, no! I don't want any of my old boyfriends coming back. They'd paddle from Cuba and show up at my doorstep if you do that. Very embarrassing for the kiddos, you know?"

"Well, I think you're a treasure. It's the world's loss. We should be hearing from people who have lived outside the U.S., people who appreciate freedom."

"Oh, they do in Cuba. They just can't tell anyone." She smiled, her mind lost in thought as she hummed a little lullaby in Spanish, moving her hips and remembering something pleasant.

"You miss it sometimes?"

"Yes and no. I miss the fictionalized version I came away with as a young girl. I don't know what it's really like, but each year, I remember the rolling parties when we used to roll the tobacco with our mothers, swat flies, and man the fans, while our overseer read stories to us. Julio Ortega. He'd been a famous fighter back in the days before the big war. Came home with one eye, and he still read to us. He was very handsome with his dark moustache, his white Fedora hat, and his cigar. We sang together. Some of us little girls danced and made our mothers laugh. The purge and the revolution were not good for our family. But before then, it was paradise. Maybe it will be again."

I always loved talking to Sandy. I also wondered what her real name was, suspecting the name was related more to a beach term than an American girl call sign.

Sandy pulled my plastic smock off and then nearly jumped. "I forgot. Your lipstick. I'm feeling orange today. How about you?"

"I could go for orange. Deep orange, though."

"Perfect with your blue."

During the broadcast, Clarence Thompson, the evening anchor, was filling in for the new morning anchor, Sylvia Torres, who announced she was pregnant with her first child about two months after she was hired. Several of my colleagues argued the spot should be given to me, since most at the station believed that Sylvia knew about her pregnancy when she was hired and was using them all.

But I had been grateful I might be given a morning time slot, which would enable me to be home with Marco at night. Until now.

Clarence's face went from a sour disposition to outright disgust, appearing to nearly vomit as the pictures of the hundreds, if not thousands, of dead fish bloating in the hot Florida sun came up. Their eyes were hollowed out by sea birds, tiny crabs, and flies, which were everywhere. Even some stingrays and unusual stingray-like prehistoric fish with long rat tails washed up that I had never seen before.

The area reporter explained matter-of-factly that the fish ate the red algae or didn't have sea glass to hide in or devour, depending on their species, due to a release of approved chemicals that were supposed to be safe for human swimmers but killed the grass.

Clarence went through two glasses of water, the last one shaking in his gnarled hand as he raised it up to his face, studded with age spots and hair plugs. He took several deep breaths and was caught on camera doing one, which would cause a scene after the show was over. Clarence would no doubt try to get the camera-man fired for having "shit for brains," which was the most common adjective he used.

"Well, Rob," I began, "thanks for that detailed re-port. I guess I won't be eating in any fish restaurants anytime soon, although—"

A noise on the other side of the podium caught my attention. Even the cameraman heard it and focused in for a headshot of Clarence Thompson throwing up all over his desk with white chunks of whatever he had for breakfast—probably oatmeal—sticking and dripping from his red tie.

I LOOKED FOR Jared Newsome, TMBC's Program Director, as I was taking off my equipment and hand-ing it to the tech on duty. I expected him to be waiting in the dark wings, stoically watching me perform with his arms crossed and his glasses shining in the dim light, not revealing his expression.

But he wasn't anywhere on the production level, so I went downstairs to Floor Five, turned the corner, and nearly crashed into Bunny Copperfield, the evening anchor gunning for Clarence's job. In fact, I had recently heard that Bunny was starting the rumors again about the older man's hands and suggestions. Clarence was stupid, especially in this day of sexual harassment, but I didn't think he was that stupid. One of these days—and it would take something more than a vomit on air—he would do something, and his career would be over. It was the price he would pay for not paying attention to the fact that while the world had moved on, he hadn't. Now his behavior, once deployed in poor taste, was something an attorney could extract a huge sum from. He didn't see it, and I wondered if he did if he wouldn't care anyway.

I bounced right off Bunny's enormous chest, which left me covered in a cloud of perfume that made my nostrils itch. Instead of reacting, all I could do was sneeze.

"So sorry, Bunny. I wasn't paying attention. That sneeze was a whopper," I lied.

"Hmph. You could hurt someone. Try paying attention, or perhaps walking more like a lady than a pirate's second in command?"

The veiled reference to Marco was kind of funny, even though her voice was laced with venom. Of all the people at the station, I trusted Bunny least of all.

Jared's door was still open, and he was standing, no doubt having just said goodbye to Bunny.

"Hey, Shannon. Sorry I didn't get up there this morning. I heard we had quite a Red Cross moment."

I rolled my eyes. "I was just glad we had socially distanced the desks, or I would be going home to change."

Jared pointed over his shoulder to the door that led to his private bathroom. "You could always use my shower. Anytime, Shannon. Anytime."

"Oh, please. Haven't you gotten tired of that, Jared? It never worked on me; it never works on anybody."

"I guess that's why you're safe to just play around with. Nothing meant by it. Don't be so prickly."

Checking my insides, I admitted my nerves for what I had to tell him were mixing things up, but I easily reeled it all in, took a deep breath, and began.

"May I sit down?"

"Absolutely." He pointed to a chair in front of his desk. He slung his right hip and thigh on the edge of the desk and leaned against it, rather than taking his rightful place behind. "What's on your mind?"

"I've decided to leave the station."

Jared stood up, hands on his hips. "What did you say?"

"I'm quitting."

"But you can't—"

"Yes, I can, and I'm going to."

"But you have a contract to fulfill. Have you forgotten that?"

"No, but that doesn't matter. I'll buy it out. And if you get nasty with this, I can always throw some dirt on Clarence. Then you can get rid of both of us."

"But I don't want to get rid of you. I was just thinking of giving you Sylvia's job during her leave. You've been wanting an anchor position. Shannon, your timing sucks."

"Marco is so busy with the Trident Towers, and we'll be going to Africa next year to start that project for the sultan. It's going to require I be available to lend a hand. And I want to do it, Jared. My priorities have changed."

"What if I doubled your salary and, say, let you go in six months? Can we arrange that?"

"Why are you so interested in giving me a shot suddenly? And do you really think money is the way to get me to stay? That was never my goal, even before I met Marco."

"I just don't want to lose you. Getting hard to find good talent. All the interns we've hired have quit, either because of Clarence or Bunny. And Bunny just gave me an ultimatum to get rid of Clarence. I'm going to do it, or I'll have to let Bunny go. Either one is going to be very sticky. You're like the one I can count on. I need you, Shannon. I really do."

"But this isn't my life any longer. I mean, don't get me wrong, it was my life. I was so looking forward to having years here, but compared to what Marco has planned, I just couldn't pass up that chance to work on these things with him. And we'll be married."

"Well, I wasn't going to ask you to give that up. I'm

not totally insane. Aren't you afraid you're not doing what you want to do? It's all for him. You're getting sucked into his world. It never was yours."

I smiled. He was good but not that good.

"You're right. When I first discussed it with Marco, I reacted a bit to the idea of quitting. Yes, I wanted my piece of the pie all my own. But look what I'd be giving up doing that. Don't you think, after years of hard work, I'd look back and say, 'You should have gone for the brass ring. You settled for second.'"

"But it's your ring. Your idea. Your vision, not Marco's. And working at this TV station is far from second. It's a huge market and a real chance to advance in the industry. You know this. Surely that has to count for something."

"But I have found a place for me inside his organization. Do you know how come I know?"

"Go ahead. I can see I'm losing this argument."

"It's because I've found a place in his heart. I love the idea of being in his shadow, having him protect and cherish me. I don't see that as anything lesser than running my own timeslot on a TV station in Tampa. It might be the world to you, but it's not for me. There's more out there. I just didn't realize it until I fell in love with him. And, yes, I thought I could do both. But I can't, Jared. Not really."

Jared stood, walked around to the back of the desk,

and took his chair. "How about just giving me time to find a replacement?"

"I don't think so."

He was good at changing the subject. "I'll bet that wedding is going to cost more than you'd earn in ten years here. Hard to compete with that kind of firepower."

"This isn't a competition. It's a choice. A chance at a glorious, adventurous life with the man I love. And, by the way, you're getting invited to the wedding."

"Oh my. I have nothing to wear."

"Do you have swim trunks and flip-flops?"

"You know I do. Not used much these days, but—"

"And your expenses will be paid—you'll get to stay in a real palace and bathe on a pink sand beach. Imagine that."

He shrugged. "Doesn't thrill me if I don't have a job to come home to."

"They'd fire you over taking a few days to go celebrate in a sultan's palace on a pink sand beach, all expenses paid?"

"Spite and envy are dangerous when you work for a female owner of your TV station."

"Nonsense. Besides, that's not just a female trait. Everyone has a little bit of that in them. We're the ones who get blamed for it, that's all. So don't come then. See how that sets with you. Tell that to your grandkids.

Tell them what you passed up. See how interesting that will sound to them."

"You gotta allow me a little wallowing. The two people I don't want are fighting over everything. The one I do want is leaving. Let's face it, I'm screwed."

"It's not that bad, Jared, and you know it. Are you really trying?"

"Trying? I'm trying harder to keep out the fruits and nuts. You wouldn't imagine the whack jobs I have coming in here. They say such stupid things. 'Oh, my grandmother thinks I'm so photogenic and she always pictures me on TV or the movies!'" he said in a starlet tone of voice. "Or guys with facelifts, blonde hair, and horrible teeth implants who are beyond their years, making me wear my sunglasses all the time their teeth are so bright. I'm wondering where all the normal people are."

"You forget, this is Tampa."

"So?"

"I think Florida attracts 'whatever goes' type of people right now. Probably won't be that way forever. You just must dig a little harder. I'd lay down the law with Clarence about the interns. And Bunny, Jared, she's not that talented. You know this, right?"

"If I fire her, would you stay on?"

It was a tempting proposal. But I had made up my mind. Before I could answer, Jared came up with another proposal.

"How about you give me just six months? I'll double your salary for six months, and during that time, I'll fire Bunny. But we can't tell anyone, okay? That will give me time to get a replacement and a good HR attorney. This was your big break, Shannon. Couldn't you find it in your heart to have a little compassion for me, the one who gave you that break? I've always treated you fairly. I just don't have the billions behind me or the body of a Greek god."

"Those aren't the reasons, and you know it."

"Find me a Wonder Woman, Shannon. I want a life like yours."

I giggled at that. "You're being silly."

"I need someone like that in my life."

I sat up straight then leaned over on the desk and stared into his eyes. "She's out there, Jared. And while you're being all miserable and envious or whatever else, she might be overlooking you, because she's looking for the same thing. People who are special don't just fly in the office window one day. You must work to attract them. Focus on what you do have, not what you don't. You'll have more takers than you can handle."

Jared wiggled his eyebrows. "I can handle a lot. So that's all I must do, make myself attractive? I thought you went after Marco. At least that's the story I was told."

I stopped at that. He was right. "Yes, I did. But there was a backstory, and that backstory was solid. Besides, I wasn't going after him to 'get' him. I wanted to see the man Emily fell in love with. I wanted to see if it was real or if I was just imagining it all. You forget, I heard lots of stories growing up. I felt like I knew him first."

He stared at me, nodding his head, perhaps afraid to say something I'd object to, so he kept quiet. It was a smart move.

I continued. "Make this place, this environment an attractive, visionary place to work. Get rid of the dead wood, the people who step on dreams."

"Clarence."

"No, Bunny."

"She's aggressive, I'll give her that."

"She's a witch, Jared. And Clarence is wounded. He's a bird with a broken wing. He's not a bad person. He's just forgotten that he has value and worth. Make him Superman. You'll find your Wonder Woman in due time, Jared. Maybe you already know her."

"I'm never going to be able to explain this conversation to a soul. I'm embarrassed to say I had this conversation with you. But thank you, Shannon. So we have a deal?"

At the risk of getting some flack at home with

Marco, I agreed to three months only. Besides, there were two golden coins in the basket Jared was offering me. First, I could finally be around to see Bunny fired, like she deserved. And second, maybe I could give enough counseling to Clarence Thompson to save his career. Neither one of them were about money nor my career, really.

It was about justice and seeing justice done. And people getting what they deserved. Maybe Marco would understand.

Just maybe.

CHAPTER 6

"**H**EY, BOSS, WE got someone from the Planning Department who says he wants to see you," Rhea said as she opened the glass door to my office.

I hoped it was good news, since I usually had to chase down officials when I needed signoffs on projects. Him coming over to the Trident office was going to save me a boatload of time.

A handsome man with a Hollywood smile entered. He was about forty, trim, with dark hair and piercing blue eyes. His smile disturbed me. I could smell a shark a mile away. It wasn't just the cologne, the pinky ring, and the custom-tailored suit that set off alarms; it was the icy cold smile trying to disguise itself as "friendly." The man had the tenacity and deliberate movements of a well-trained serial killer. Nails buffed, shoes polished, no wrinkles or creases out of place on his white shirt under the shiny navy-blue suit.

And then his voice cinched it.

"Sorry to come barging in here, Mr. Gambini," he said in a slightly Eastern European accent, but I wasn't sure.

I extended my hand for the shake, which also confirmed my suspicions since the man nearly liberated me from his fingers until I twisted his wrist at an awkward angle, as if examining the expensive watch at the base of the man's hand, which caused a slight crack in one of the little bones and caused the man some pain. I was sure of that.

"I'm a great admirer of a man who wears the finest watches, Mr.—"

"Sivic. This is Theopolis Sivic." Rhea stared down at the card and frowned but continued, "Independent Regional Planning Director."

"Ah, private contractor. You are not a county employee then?"

"No, I have more authority," Sivic said coolly as he withdrew his hand and tried not to show the pain he was experiencing.

I knew I'd won round one, but a wounded bear was always twice as dangerous.

The gentleman straightened his spine, pressed his shoulders back, and shook his arms to allow the fine fabric of his suit to readjust unwrinkled. He pulled on his cuffs, one at a time, as if he was trimming fat on a good steak, inhaled, and stared back at me.

Challenge accepted, asshole.

I counted five for his box breathing and let the gentleman make the first move. I'd be ready.

"I have been retained by the City of Belleair Beach on behalf of her citizens."

Yeah, I'll bet you're careful with the ladies. You're still an asshole.

"I've been asked to look into the allegations that certain liberties have been taken with the change in plans for your Trident Towers project—contracts that involved local workers that will not now be honored in favor of construction crews from out of the area. Your approval and contract with the city states—"

"Excuse me, how do you know what my contract and development agreement states? That information is supposed to be confidential."

"Ah, yes, but that doesn't apply in the case of fraud or misuse of public funds. You've been given a density bonus, allowing you to build an additional twenty-three units added on your latest plan. But it's a conditional approval. It provides for the provision that you do your best to hire local contractors—"

"They are local. You're mistaken."

"But we have it—"

"I don't care where you have it or how you carry it. You're simply wrong."

"Would you please demonstrate to me why?"

"I don't have to. This doesn't concern me, and you've illegally obtained copies of my development plan. I don't even know if this card," I tossed it on the desk, "is legitimate."

"I see. So you are going to make this a fight." His eyes searched mine dangerously. The man was not only slimy and cunning, but he was also mean. I saw one telltale scar on the bridge of his nose, which looked like an injury not quite repaired seamlessly. His blue orbs begged for a physical confrontation. They twinkled, almost iridescent, anxious for action.

"I have no reason to fight you. I have no reason to pay any attention to you. Get out of my office immediately, or I'll do my cop buddies a favor and toss you out myself."

Rhea was no stranger to yelling and anger, but her eyes were wide, her mouth dropping to her chest as she looked between the two men both itching to prove themselves. Behind her, a room full of my team had stopped whatever they were doing mid-motion and looked equally disturbed.

I wanted to smile at her to give her some confidence but didn't want to take his eyes off Mr. Sivic. But he saw the room out of the corner of his eye and noticed the lack of motion, the phones going unanswered, as if some God had stopped all time in its tracks while Sivic and I were still breathing.

Sivic was going to speak when something happened I did not expect. Rebecca sauntered in through the office, looking right and left with casual distain at workers who, if they knew her, hated every cell in her body. She wore a bright orange ruffled dress knee-high, with little multicolored abstract shapes dotting all over the fabric, as it swayed easily with the movement of her hips. Her very long legs were fully exposed to her mid-thigh when she stepped forward due to a large slit on either side of the front panel. Her fingernails and toes were orange this time and matched her new hair color: Lucille Ball red.

She slipped her lithe body next to Sivic's, delicately pushed her arm through the crook of his right elbow, and leaned into him so I could see Sivic's upper arm remained buried in her breasts. She even gave a little shameless moan.

How in the world could I have ever latched on to this vampire? What was I thinking? Oh yes, I wasn't thinking. I was looking for intensity, something to obliterate the pain.

She was repulsive to me, and I didn't mind showing it.

"I've been waiting to talk to you again. Have you not gotten my messages?" she asked, coyly, turning, nearly engulfing Sivic's hand in her crotch. I enjoyed the little parade because I finally saw Sivic's breaking point, that twitch in his left eye and the pulsing vein in his forehead. He was uncomfortable with the display.

I pulled my eyes off the struggling Sivic, who was now suddenly less bold in the presence of the emasculator, *Rebecca the Terrible*. I nodded to Rhea.

"We're fine here. Let's bring in an extra chair, and we'll have our meeting in my office." I sat, looked up at the two standing before me, and asked, "Would anyone like coffee, tea, or some wine?" I blinked a couple of times to keep myself from stifling a giggle, even though I knew I was going to be handed a pile of shit.

"I-I'll have coffee," said Sivic. "Just black, please." He turned to Rhea, whose eyes expanded nearly to her ears.

"Thanks, Rhea. Rebecca?" I craned his neck up.

"I like pink champagne. *Sophia*, was it that? Our anniversary champagne." She smiled, but it was cut short by my comment.

"Sorry, I don't remember any of that. But I think we might have some. Right, Rhea?"

"I think so, Boss. You want some Sparkle?"

"Love some."

When Rhea closed the door in front of her and turned to the rest of the office, everyone scampered like mice, not wanting to admit they'd been glued to the action inside my office like a good series on TV.

I checked my phone for messages and silently waited for Rebecca and Sivic to take a seat and begin their no-doubt rehearsed presentation.

Rhea mercifully didn't take long to bring the drinks. I avoided direct eye contact with Rebecca, something I knew would drive her crazy. She whispered things to Sivic, at one point, making him chuckle. I found it easy to ignore them. I sipped my sparkling lemon drink, folded my hands on my desk, and sighed.

"I'm sure we all are busy, so can we get down to it?" I directed my gaze to the space between Rebecca and Sivic, making the younger man turn and check behind him. "Everything you have to say could have been said through an attorney or with an email or letter. I don't understand the need for the meeting in person. I have nothing against you, Theopolis—if I may call you that?"

"Of course. Most people call me Theo. That's fine as well, Mr. Gambini."

"Then it has to be Marco."

"And Marco it is."

I deduced Rebecca was annoyed that the two men were building rapport and she was being left out. Her flowery dress with the plunging neckline was in constant motion, and she crossed and uncrossed her legs several times, showing off her orange toe polish and jeweled sandals. I found I had no emotion when it came to her. No regrets, no images of happy days in the past. It was a fifteen-year blur, a prison sentence from which I'd been liberated.

"I'm going to say it one more time. I'm busy. I'm sure, with your important job, Theo, you are as well. What seems to be the issue at hand?"

Sivic began explaining that formal approval of the Trident Towers did not have legal authority. It was going to require he bring the project before the planning commission, which was booked up for nearly four months. He said that continued work on the development could create fines for every one of the violations. He promised that there were many of them.

"Well, that's going to be a disappointment to my partners," I stated calmly. I took another sip of my Sparkle and watched Rebecca's shaky hand deliver the champagne to her gut at the same time.

"Partners?" she asked, frowning.

"The Department of Veterans Affairs. They have a stake in this, and I understand they have jurisdiction over local laws. I also don't understand how you could determine I'm in violation of the labor clauses of our development agreement since we have not yet begun work."

"We understand you are employing labor from India. We have it on good authority these individuals are being smuggled into the country without passports," Sivic neatly laid out.

"So you are under contract with the State Department as well? Impressive, if I do say so myself," I said, raising my eyebrows. "If what you say is true, I will contact Senator Campbell and ask for his assistance to this oversight. You know he is married to the First Lady's sister?"

Sivic briefly glanced at Rebecca and then remembered himself. "We are going by sworn affidavits."

"Which are not worth the paper they're written on, even if they do exist. Look, I'm growing tired of doing this waltz. You aren't going to win."

"But we can make it very expensive, Marco," Rebecca hissed.

"Why? So you can take away a chance for a normal life with vets that have served their country well and have been forgotten? You want to take away their pride, their future? The comfort of a home over their heads to share with their children while they crawl their way back into society with dignity? Everyone else sees them as heroes. What's gotten into you that you can't see this is a losing proposition?"

"I'm not fond of losing, or have you forgotten?"

I drilled her a look that was deep and dark. "Don't fuck with me, Rebecca. I didn't like it when you pretended to be in love with me. I like it less now that we are sworn enemies. You have no right to do this."

She set her stemware on my desk, admiring it, her fingers running up and down the graceful stem with the etched pattern near the top. "I see you still have our crystal. Does it bring back memories?"

"No." I hadn't remembered they were. I was going to throw them all away, these at the office and the two I had at home. "Why, Rebecca?"

"Because I can."

"I can do a lot of things, but I don't do them. For one, it would send me to jail, but for another, I don't go chasing windmills or ghosts from my past. I can't help it if you were raped at your father's horse ranch or that you cannot have children. Perhaps therapy would be a more agreeable solution, and I can recommend any number of therapists to help you with that troubled mind of yours. I'll even pay for it."

"Just a minute, Marco—Mr. Gambini," Sivic blurted out, placing his arm across Rebecca as if protecting her from the onslaught of Marco's words. "This is a civil discussion."

"Is it? You can't give me a reason all this is befalling

me and my organization? You call that civil? Messing with me? I've done nothing wrong. You might consider your own options, Mr. Sivic. This is what happens when you end a relationship with Rebecca. Ask yourself: Is this what I want? There are several gentlemen of good reputation who bailed. Just something to think about."

"You're taking this too personal, Mr. Gambini."

"Am I? Then ask her why she's doing this. See if you can get a straight answer from her. I could shout it from the rooftops. I'll go to the tabloids if I must. I've got more information on her cold, perverted world than anyone else out there." I drilled another hateful stare into her. "I'm the one who deserves revenge. You're the one who left and took everything. You got what you wanted, so get out and leave me alone. You can't have what isn't yours."

Sivic was blathering about getting a cease-and-desist order when Rebecca cut him off.

"I need to talk to Marco alone."

"I don't think that's a good—"

"Get out, and I won't ask you again."

I knew I'd rattled her cage, and if I wasn't careful, I'd allow myself too much pleasure at her expense, part of the dark sexual games she liked to play. And it would sully me, not her. So I reeled my emotions back inside.

My tone was soothing, like I was reassuring a favorite dog. "Theo, give us just a moment. I'm sure it will be all right. Just a minute." I watched as Sivic left the office, but he took up a chair outside and watched through the window. Team workers stared at each other, confused and worried. They kept their distance from the strange, obsessed man.

I began. "I'm not going to play along with this. Tell me what you want. Is it more money? What will it take for you to get out of my life altogether and never come back?"

"I made a mistake walking out. I'd like the opportunity to make it up to you."

I was stunned.

"I do tend to bite the hand that feeds me. I'm sorry for that. I've recently come to the realization that I need you, Marco. I need your strength. I miss your fucks worse than you can imagine. I'm baring my soul to you. I'm a wreck without you."

The words sounded hollow. I knew it was all lies, part of the game. Catch the mouse, injure it a bit, let it go free, and then capture it again, each time doing more and more damage, even licking its wounds, before the final crunch or a "natural" death. The term "Cat and Mouse" was only a partial description. It was more like something from Dante's Inferno.

I inhaled carefully and continued. "This, this is how you ask for sympathy?"

"Because I know you won't give it. I'm not asking. I'm demanding."

"You're insane, Rebecca. I should have you arrested and—" I was seeing another side of her entirely. A very unbalanced and dangerous side. I knew she could smell my fear too. She was a predator. I was a protector. It was going to be a fight to the death. Her mind had completely unwound.

"Rebecca, don't destroy the last ounce of respect I once had for you with this. Get some help. This is a suicide mission. You'll take a lot of innocents down with you. And you'll still lose. Are you there, still there, Rebecca?"

I wasn't going to allow myself to feel sorry for her, but I was a fair man, a man of compassion, which made me feel proud. Rebecca had become an animal and probably was well on her way to full insanity.

I asked again, "Are you taking anything? Is there an underlying problem I don't know about?"

"You see the shame in admitting all this? I was counting on you having something left for me."

I shook my head. "I care about you as a person. But you've done some horrible things, things that have cost people jobs, cost me millions. You delayed a project that was near and dear to my heart. Even if I had anything left, I have a new life now. I've moved on. There is no place for you here."

"I could make one."

A cold chill slithered down my spine.

"What did you say?"

"I thought you needed me as much as I needed you. I thought you needed that intensity we had together. I wanted the biggest make up fuck of my lifetime. But it didn't work out that way."

I saw the imbalance taking over her. I leaned slightly to the left and made eye contact with Sivic, who stood, waiting to be invited in.

"What's your freedom worth to you?" she asked.

I could almost see a snake's tongue protruding from her mouth—all my imagination.

"I'm sorry, Rebecca. I'm not following you." I looked at her hands, her purse, her pockets, suddenly fearful she might be carrying a small caliber revolver. "Are you using something because you're not making any sense. There is absolutely nothing you could do—"

I hated myself for this slip of the tongue. That's the last thing I should have said, because Rebecca stood up and ended their conversation with—

"Think about it. Is your freedom worth the life of

someone very dear to you?"

"Rebecca, you can't mean that—"

"Can lightning strike twice?"

CHAPTER 7

I GOT HOME early and was preparing one of Marco's favorite meals: lean steak, garlic mashed potatoes, and string beans, heavy with butter. For dessert, I made fresh custard with half the sugar, just as Marco liked it. It was simple, reflecting the man and his modest tastes beneath his complicated body armor, but it was the basis on which my love found safety, a firm foundation built on rock and concrete, like his buildings. Not built on sand.

I'd had an exhausting day at the office, especially avoiding anyone who had reason to interact with me, except Sandy, of course. Clarence was on his good behavior, and I asked him if he'd like to have a late lunch after my weather report at noon tomorrow. He delightedly accepted.

With twinkling eyes, like a kid at Christmas, he asked, "To what do I owe this kind gesture?"

"I want us to have a talk and understand something," I answered.

He quickly looked down at his feet. "Oh."

Apparently, he'd had lots of these types of conversations, I guessed.

"It's not what you think, Clarence. I want us to work together, but I first want to set up the ground rules. I want you to be perfectly clear where I'm coming from. If you pay attention, you'll avoid something that's coming your way that you're unprepared for."

He turned his head to the side as if he could hear better from his left ear. "Sounds serious. Dark and delicious."

The waving of his eyebrows was unnecessary and annoyed me. *Are you really that clueless?*

"I'll drive and drop you back here well in time for your evening preparation," I said.

"I don't mind the distraction. It would be my honor—" He reached out to grab my hand for a Victorian kiss, and I stepped back.

"No. That's partly what I'm going to talk to you about. Part of the rules."

He adjusted his body and looked up to the sky as his fingers mimicked rain. "Okay, okay, no touchy, no touchy."

I thought about that as I sliced the green beans and set the water to boil on the stove. Marco would be home any minute, or he'd call.

I dashed to our tiny bedroom, removed the robe I'd worn after taking my second shower of the day, and added some fancy underwear. The new crotchless panties and a matching bra that exposed my nipples made my privates pulse in anticipation. I used a slight spray of Audrey Hepburn's favorite recipe perfume, directing it mostly at the back of my neck and beneath my ears, and then spread a thin layer of cherry gel over my nipples and my private parts.

I didn't consider it to be manipulation but was going to need all the help I could get as I tried to explain to him about the fact that I'd disobeyed his command. If I let him take it out on me sexually, it might remove some of the sting. But I wasn't sure. All this was new territory. I wanted to be compliant but not a victim begging for mercy. A planned supplicant, showing my need for him to be master of my life because I'd done a course correction he might not agree with. I wanted to sweeten my indiscretion with a little sugar, a little salt, and a whole lot of passion.

I placed the silk robe back on and cinched the tie with a bow. Candles were lit. A bottle of red wine was opened and waiting on the table, along with two beautiful pieces of stemware he'd commandeered from the office. The water was hot, covered, waiting. The broiler was not yet on, but the steaks were marinating on a platter, properly peppered and lightly salted. The mashed potatoes were already done and sitting with a dollop of butter melting sensually into the peaks and valleys of the white and red-skinned fluffiness.

The ocean was a bit angry with white caps and a sky that was turning dark grey, meaning it would rain tonight or sooner. The sunset would still be later, depending on how many of the monstrous clouds joined them in the next hour.

Marco's Hummer pulled into the Beach Trail Drive parking spot next to my car, and I heard the door open.

Something strange was in his expression, almost like regret as he quickly scanned my outfit, the table set for him, and then looked away.

I knew better than to press things but did it anyway.

"You look like a whole lot of good news walking in here like that."

"Sorry I don't meet your standards," he whispered, setting down a sheaf of papers. He looked over at the table again and sighed. "I guess my timing sucks."

"There's nothing at all wrong with your timing. You're going to have to work harder if you think you can brush me off like that. Stop hiding. What is it?"

His shoulders dropped as he exhaled. "Shannon, I can't. I have to think about a few things first."

I walked over to him, and he did begin to smile

then. I figured he smelled my perfume and knew I'd made myself extra pleasing for his behalf. I acknowledged that he liked it, or normally liked it.

"You don't have to do a thing, Marco. Just sit down, and I'll take your shoes off. Your feet must be hurting. Can I rub them?"

He angled his head and then looked deep into my eyes and let me know his intention was there, even if his will was lacking. I got the message.

"Let's see what I can do."

He started to say something, and I placed my palm over his lips, bending over so he could see the gap in my robe. Then I knelt and began to slip off his shoes and socks, only worn today because he had meetings with bankers, he'd told me.

"Those poor little toes," I said as I manipulated them back and forth, gently rubbing the underside of both his feet. I leaned forward, knees to the area rug beside his toes. One shoulder became exposed as the rob slipped slightly.

I massaged his calves through his slacks, then used my knuckles to trace the ribbons of sinew on his thighs. I reached for his shirt and began to unbutton them one at a time while he watched me carefully. I noticed his breathing was getting deeper. My forearm brushed against the bulge growing in his pants and I ignored it.

I spread his shirt open but didn't remove it from his arms. Next, I lifted his tee shirt to expose his chest and the bulging abs and pecs moving up and down with his slow breathing.

Coming to my feet, I relaxed onto the leather couch, placing my knees at the sides of his waist and unbuckled his belt, releasing him to my deft fingers.

Marco sat up straight, inhaled, and overcame my mouth, sending his tongue down my throat, making my sex drip with desire. He pulled my hair aside and bit my earlobe then kissed my neck. With his other hand, he worked with mine to slide his pants down off his hips just enough so he was fully free.

His fingers went to slide the panties to the side for a quick, urgent entry, but he soon discovered it wasn't needed. With both hands on my hips, he watched as my body covered his lap and he held me down, deep, then moved my frame up and down his shaft. I untied my robe and showed him my rosy, red nipples knotted and begging to be kissed, pressing above the black lace of the bra, engorging them dangerously.

He lifted my leg up over the armrest of the couch to widen his access to me. I locked my hands behind his neck, squeezed my breasts together as he buried his head there. He sucked, grunting his pleasure, stopping his hip action several times to cool his arousal. But I would not be stopped. I moaned and begged for him, trying to come down on him again, but he seemed to enjoy restraining me.

At last, he pulled me down and urgently stroked my insides, building up to a hot crescendo with such ferocity he flipped me on my back, tore off his shirt and pants, and rammed inside me again, making me squeal with delight. He rolled and pinched my nipples and then sucked them back to softness. He pulled my bra straps down to my elbows, unhooked the back and freed my breasts as he arched, pumping with quick little hip motions while my insides flamed and started to pulse.

I arched up to receive him, but he lost traction in my lumpy couch when one knee slipped to the floor. He slipped his arm beneath my back and flipped me over again, bringing me on all fours and mounting me from the backside, pulling my hips tight against him as he squeezed my butt cheeks apart, which sent me into orbit. After just a few more strokes, my orgasm began to roll through me, shaking my body as my internal muscles held and stroked him in return.

"Never. Want. This. To. End," he whispered in my ear, as I pressed against him, rose with him to my knees, gripping the backrest of the couch until I felt him begin to spill. He held my shaking body as he poured into me, taking me deep, nearly lifting me with an arm around my belly, drilling inside, demanding to stay, holding me still so we could both feel the friction of flesh against flesh until we melted into the miracle of our combined union.

It was over too soon for me. My heart was still roaring as he slowed his pace, placing grateful kisses up and down my spine, splaying his fingers through my hair, and finding parts he'd missed kissing earlier at the back of my ears, at the nape of my neck, and down every vertebra.

We collapsed, sitting side by side, my robe halfway under me and halfway on the ground beneath our feet, breathing in tandem until I could inhale without gasping. I leaned my head against his shoulder, my hand gently stroking his chest, then kissed him under his chin. He wrapped his arms around me and let me just breathe in the warmth of his embrace. Leaning my cheek against him, I listened to the steady beat of his heart.

I was satisfied that whatever had been troubling Marco when he walked in through my door was now safely forgotten. Or at least I hoped it was.

He cleared the hair from my forehead, pressing strands behind my ear to look into my eyes. A tiny dark cloud remained there.

"What is it, Marco?"

"I am the happiest man alive, Shannon. I'm just grateful."

There was something else, but he wasn't going to reveal it, and I didn't want to spoil the glow I felt all over. "Me too," I said and placed my forehead against his. "Can I suggest some dinner perhaps?"

"You think my heart could stand it?"

"It's steak. Good for your libido. Not oysters, mind you, but nearly as effective. Garlic mashed potatoes, string beans, and dessert too. Are you ready?"

He gazed down at his shirt and pants. "I think I ruined my shirt."

"Oh dear. I liked how you got carried away. So sorry about the shirt, though."

"I'm not." He smiled. "Come on. I'm starved. I'll grab some pajama bottoms, but you can stay just the way you are."

I smiled, disobeying him again by wrapping the robe around me and cinching the waist while he retrieved his pajamas from the bedroom. We walked to the table I'd set, the candles still lit, the flowers I'd bought still standing, waiting for attention.

While I fixed the beans and put the steaks in the broiler, he replaced the wine glasses with two juice tumblers for some strange reason and handed me a glass.

"To endless nights of good food, good wine, wonderful stories to think back upon and remember how perfect we are together. The perfect pairing," he said.

"I agree." I clinked my glass against his. "What did you do with the wine glasses?"

"I like these better." He sipped, closing his eyes. "The wine tastes better in these."

I took a sip, closed my eyes, and let the taste roll over my tongue and call to me. "Yes, I think you're right." I was going to say more, but he'd covered my mouth with his, his hand squeezing my right breast.

The smell of our steaks cooking refocused our attention to plating our food and sitting down, finally.

Toward the end of the meal, he asked me about my day at the station, which immediately put me on the defensive. His questions were answered with vague or one-word answers, until he finally put down his knife and fork and sat back in his chair with his hands folded in his lap.

His face was serious. "Tell me," he said.

I knew better than to try to hide something from him. But the evening had been so wonderful I didn't want to spoil it. I trusted him with the truth, hoping I'd not miscalculated.

"I met with Jared today to put in my resignation."

"And?" He watched me, not resuming his eating.

"And I didn't quit."

"But that wasn't the plan, Shannon. You promised you would quit. I haven't asked you about it until today. And today you chickened out?"

"No, I decided to give him three months to find a replacement."

There. I'd said it. I continued eating.

"Impossible. There is no possibility he could replace you in a year or even two."

"Not just me. He's going to fire Bunny."

"And keep Clarence."

"Yes, I told him to."

"That's another bad decision. Who cares if he must replace all three of you? In my opinion, neither Bunny nor Clarence is doing anything for the station. In fact, they're hurting it. You're the only bright spot there."

"They have a new hire who's going on maternity leave. Sylvia. She'll be good."

"This manager of yours hires a new anchorperson who's pregnant, leaves an aging beauty queen in the position to boss everyone around and scare half the crew, and coddles an aging Casanova who drools and vomits over himself at the sight of dead fish. Have I got that right?"

I wanted to laugh because Marco was spot on and making very funny sense, too. "You make it sound like it's the Little Shop of Horrors or something."

"That's an apt description," he said brightly, holding up his fork and stabbing another slice of steak. "You're needed here, beside me, to help me with our plans. Our plans, Shannon. They're not my plans.

They're ours."

"Yes, I understand that. But, Marco, I told him I'd give him three months *and* we agreed I'd cut back my hours. It's what I thought was the right thing to do. He's been good to me, Marco. I can't just leave him in the lurch. I'm sorry if you're angry with me." I placed a hand on his. "Please understand."

"Oh, I understand all right. This postpones everything I'm doing then. Am I to believe you're okay with that?"

"No. Like I said, I'm cutting back my hours. No evening or afternoon anchor fill-ins. Just weather and an occasional story in the morning, working with Sylvia, not Clarence. He and Bunny can duke it out in the evenings. I'm out of that scene. I'll be with you more. I'll be home or back at the office three, four hours earlier, and if you have a trip, I'll take off from the station, no problem. He agreed to that. All of that."

His face got dark again.

"Marco, what is troubling you so?"

He put down his fork again and pushed away from the table but remained seated. "I've spoken to our new Security Chief. He's worried about your stalker."

"I'm not going to jog in the morning. Not alone, anyway."

"That's a start. But in addition to the classes, we're going to beef up our security in general—everywhere.

Our office is too open. We need to run it like the station does. And I need to keep you protected."

"You think there's a threat to me?"

"We do believe there's a credible threat. Yes."

His eyes were cloudy again. They quickly diverted from my questioning gaze and didn't connect.

"What else?"

Marco threw his napkin on the table. "Dammit, Shannon. Can't you see I'm trying to take good care of you? It's my job to do that, but it's just something that I couldn't live with if—"

"If what?"

"If someone were to try something."

"As in harm me?"

He stood, walking to the large slider overlooking the beach. The moon danced amongst the large puffy white clouds in the night sky. I followed the trail of a string of cotton balls as they blew past us both. He knew I loved this house. Was he saying I'd need a posted armed guard at my back patio? Front door?

"I get the concern and the need to get all the information, but why does this make you angry? I don't understand your reaction. I'm asking normal questions, Marco. And if there's a plot against me, why should I be left in the dark? Shouldn't I be told these things?"

He turned around and nodded. "Yes, you're right."

He retook his seat, held my hand, and began again to say something he did not want to tell me, and that made me fearful.

"We've analyzed it, Shannon. We think Rebecca might try to harm you. We have no proof, just theory. Promise me you'll alter what you do, and perhaps we'll assign a guard for you as well. If I can't be there around you twenty-four seven, someone else has to be."

"Did you run into Rebecca today?"

He rubbed the knuckles on my hand, and nodded.

"And she admitted it, that she might harm me?"

"It was an indirect implication. I've already done some of the research, and it isn't enough to get a restraining order against her."

"So she isn't on some island with her future Mr. Ex-Rebecca like you told me."

"She means to delay our project. No, she's not given up. Now do you understand why I need you where I can watch over you? Don't you see how important it is?"

I couldn't believe Rebecca would rise to that level, but if Marco did, that would be proof enough. He was the expert.

No wonder he was in such a dour mood when he arrived home.

"So what do we do?"

"We can go into all that tomorrow, Shannon. I'm

still working on it. And frankly, I'm tired."

So much for romance, I thought. Just when it all was feeling so perfect, limitless, with so much to live for, to work for, so much good that we could do together, someone would try to dash those dreams and get to him in the worst possible way. Rebecca had figured out his Achilles heel.

And was crazy enough to try to use it.

"But why, Marco? What's she about?"

"I think she's mentally unbalanced. I'm not sure how, but I'm going to get her exposed and try to take care of it that way. Clinically. But I won't lie to you. It's a slippery slope, and we must be very careful, or it could cause a lawsuit. She's still got a lot of my money to throw back at my face with attorneys. We've been duped, I'm afraid. She's been summoning her troops."

I was crestfallen. I picked up the dishes, rinsing them in the sink, and began putting them in the dishwasher. He came up behind me, encircling me in his arms, and whispered, "I'll figure out a way. I promise to love and protect you, and I'll spare no expense figuring this thing out. I don't want you to worry. I just need you to play smart and keep your eyes and ears open. Remember what I told you about evil? Well, evil doesn't sleep. Crazy people don't sleep, either."

I remembered what we'd talked about many times,

that love was stronger than hate. And the enemy would always think that I was the weakest link.

I wasn't going to let that happen. And I wasn't going to take anything for granted, either. It was ridiculous to allow it to ruin a beautiful evening with the man I'd love forever. And if I had to, I'd fight to make it last forever.

But I had to get ready for it first.

Marco interrupted my thoughts.

"Come on. It's time for bed. We can finish the rest of this in the morning." He took my hand and walked me to the bedroom.

"Shower?"

I nodded.

He smoothed the lavender gel all over my body, washing every part of me diligently. He took great pains to hose me off, again smoothing his scarred and massive fingers over my flesh, making my arousal flash in waves. Everywhere he touched me, even if he violated me, I glowed. Wanted more.

I threw my arms around his neck, allowed him to hold me under the warm spray, and sobbed into his chest.

He was my lifeline. I would do or say anything to protect him as he would for me. He was like a drug, and I became more and more addicted to him with every passing day, every time our bodies touched, fondled, and made love.

When I was done, he spoke softly. "We'll figure it out one step at a time. I'm going to remain calm, logical. I need you to keep your head about you too. There must be an answer to all this. It's just not coming to me right away, but it's there."

"I know you will. I want to help. And I'll follow your lead and instructions."

"Thank you, Shannon. Thank you for trusting me."

I winced, tried to engage his attention, and then put my palms on his cheeks. "Except for the station. I need those three months partly to help us with the social media and press we're going to need, Marco. I know what I'm doing."

"You're even more stubborn than Em—I'm sorry, it just slipped out."

"It's okay. I don't mind that I remind you of her. I'm actually quite honored, flattered."

"For being stubborn?" He gave me back a puzzled look.

I kissed him again under the water. "Thank you for letting me be me. Thank you for telling me the truth."

But something was at the tip of his tongue, and he wouldn't let it out. I finally asked him as the water turned cold.

While drying my head under the towel, I told him, "You know you can confide in me anything. Anything at all, Marco."

He stopped for a minute. "All in due time. I have some things I must sort out, but yes, after I organize my thoughts and create a plan, I'll share it with you. All of it. I won't leave anything out. I'm going to get the very best people on it, and we'll come up with a plan that will work."

"Then nothing can stop us. No problem too great that we cannot handle when we're together. Make me believe that we'll live this way for the next hundred years and that it will keep getting better and better."

"It will, Shannon. I promise it will. Love is stronger than evil. It always wins in the end."

"No matter what."

"No matter what. There is nothing that can separate us. I will never let that happen."

CHAPTER 8

I DROVE SHANNON to the station myself because her car wouldn't start. I had a repairman stop by the house, to see if he could get it jumped and fixed by tonight. I never minded being her chauffeur, and it was part of the plan anyway.

"I just had it serviced a month ago. It has less than ten thousand miles on it," she complained as we headed for the station. "I was supposed to have lunch with Clarence."

"I can't make it for lunch. Ask him to reschedule. I don't want you driving with anyone else."

"Aren't we being a little too dramatic?" she asked.

"Shannon, we talked all about this last night. I thought I made it perfectly clear that we're beefing up security. This isn't a joke, you know."

"I've never had any trouble with this car."

"You probably left your lights on or the radio," I answered.

"They aren't like that now. Even my cheap little car shuts off the lights or anything electronic when the engine has been turned off."

I reassured her that it was probably something very simple as we sped down the highway to the bridge over the bay, headed to downtown Tampa.

We arrived. I kissed her goodbye, and after she went upstairs to get her makeup done, I slipped into Jared's office. I knocked with my knuckles on the open door's frame. Jared had so much paperwork covering his desk, his two guest chairs, and the upturned waste-paper basket he looked like a hamster making a nest. Even the floor was littered with files I carefully wandered around.

"Ah, the man himself. The maid's got the day off," Jared said, peering through glasses perched at the tip of his nose. He stood, and the we shook.

"Shannon told me about your little arrangement."

"You put her up to it. Don't blame this on her," barked Jared. His phone rang and he couldn't find it under all the papers. When he did, the ringing stopped. Checking the number first, he tossed it on top of one of his piles.

"I don't think you need a maid. You need a bull-dozer. We used to have a liaison in the SEALs with a desk that looked like yours. He was always complaining that he never got the memos everyone else did when, in fact, he'd buried them. Until, of course, they were no longer pertinent. We thought it was his strategy all along, that way he only had to do half the work for the same amount of pay."

"I take it he didn't advance."

"Secret is, you have to stay in long enough so you can coast. You can't pull these things off while you're essential. When you get kicked upstairs, that sometimes means you're not needed. The Navy doesn't fire people; they promote them. All the branches are the same. The brass at the top depend on the grunts to get the work done, under pain of detachment. But once you've ridden up the food chain a bit, you never had to worry about that. He started slowing down too soon, and yes, he got sent to Alaska to run a supply warehouse that supported the SEALs training up there."

"Not exactly Coronado."

"Nope. No coeds, no warm ocean breezes, palm trees, or beach volleyball."

"That's a fuckin' sad story, Marco. What was the point of it?"

"Hell if I know."

We both laughed as worthy sometimes-adversaries.

"What can I do to convince you to let her go early, like in a week or two, maybe tonight?" I asked.

"Funny. I was just going to ask you the same thing."

I picked up a sheaf of papers on a chair and set them on the floor beside me as I sat in front of Jared. "But there is something you can do, and you never know how deep my gratitude can go. What do you know about my ex?"

"Rebecca? Shannon's the one who interviewed her, not me."

"A tall, handsome Program Manager who decides what leads and what goes and the butterfly from hell attracted to publicity like her life depended on it. That sounds like a perfect match made in Heaven, Jared."

"That's a blood sport. I don't have the stomach."

"She can wear on you. She can be charming if she wants to."

"Now you've just about explained every woman on the planet. Oh—I forgot. You're still in the 'honeymoon' phase," he said, emphasizing it with his fingers making quote marks. "Blinded by love."

"I am hopelessly in love. And I have my own ideas what I'd like to do with Shannon, which means anyone who gets in the way is a problem for me. You wouldn't have it in you to play a little cat and mouse?"

"You must be fuckin' nuts, Marco. She's like this wild two-hundred-pound mountain lion, and I'm one of those little pink feeder mice with his eyes still shut. That would be no contest. One gulp and Jared would be no more. Can't you find one of your former SEAL buddies who might be just a little bent in the bedroom, if you know what I mean? I understand she has tastes that are difficult to satisfy."

I stared him down.

Jared stood, holding his hands out in front of him. "Just a rumor, Marco. I have no first-hand experience."

"I'm looking for a favor here, Jared."

"No, to be quite frank, you're wanting to send me on a suicide mission."

"Then find a way to get some information on her. I want to know why she won't leave me alone. She's beginning to worry me."

"Now you're worried? After all you've been through?"

"I need to know what she's planning."

"Marco, she's not going to tell me."

Jared did look like a skinny mouse, I thought. Shannon had told me how many times he'd asked her out, even after it was discovered she was with me. It was a "feel sorry for me date" I had been trying to set up, on the chance that an opportunity might present itself.

But then I had an idea.

"What if she thought she could get inside information from you about me, through your working relationship with Shannon? If she thought you were useful, she'd let you live for a bit."

"You instill such confidence, Marco. I'm not inter-ested in living for a bit. I'd like to live to an old age and die comfortably in my bed. No. The answer is no. This would be too rich for me. I'm not smart enough, I don't have the cunning or the stealth you have, and I'll get nervous and blow it. I'm the last person in the world you'd want to use."

"I think you're wrong."

Jared fell back into his chair again, staring off to the right, not making eye contact. "This is the part where you threaten to kill my mother and my sisters. Then you'll firebomb the station, and I'd be spectacularly out of a job. The whole thing caught on camera and presented to the Tampa market by *someone else's* TV station."

"We could help you make some improvements. Get you in on the ground floor of the Trident Towers, interviewing happy vets being given what they deserve. You'd have exclusive interviews, and then imagine the talent who would come calling? Bone Frog Develop-ment could become one of your best advertisers. Your owner would love that."

Jared suddenly looked very small, tucked into his enormous chocolate brown high-backed office swivel chair. "Might even get you a real secretary to have this place looking like Fox in no time at all. If we were going to interview Tom Brady, you'd have to do a substantial remodel, and of course, you'd need season tickets for ten in your box seats."

"None of this would be remotely important to me if I was roadkill, Marco. You know I'm no match for her. You could give me the sun and the moon. I don't even know what the hell I'd do with them. You do see, the answer is still no."

I continued nodding as I stood, leaned over, and shook Jared's hand again. "Well, it was nice having a little fantasy with you. But you think it over. If you come across something you just can't live without, you let me know. Ever been on a safari? We're taking some people over there in the spring."

"Just my kind of place. I've always wanted to vacation in West Africa with all those exciting macho Jeep jockeys running around cutting the heads off people who look like me. That's you're style, not mine."

I chuckled. "You're funny, Jared. I think you could have done standup comedy."

"Let's add that to the list then, shall we? Just another missed opportunity."

The standoff was beginning to annoy me. I wasn't used to being told, "No". But I knew that if Shannon and I spent enough time on it, we'd discover Jared's weakness.

And then we'd be home free.

But we had to come up with something he'd risk

his life for to get.

ON MY WAY over to the office, I got a call from Harry, the Sultan of Bonin's youngest son, from Brooklyn Heights. Harry had become the trusted social secretary to the sultan, his father. He lived with his mother, the beautiful Salima, the sultan's favorite companion. Since she was from a servant family and not nobility, he could not make her his wife. She was sent away along with her illegitimate son, for their own safety. The sultan gave her a stipend and purchased a brownstone for her as long as she lived. The rest of the harem wives and children pretended not to know this or openly admit that Harry was their relative.

"Marco, are you ready for the princes?" Harry barked over the phone.

"Are they here?"

"They land in New York in about an hour. Then there's the plane to Charlotte and finally Tampa. They will arrive this evening around ten if everything goes well. But we might have some issues. Do you want me to arrange a car?"

"That would be nice, Harry. Thanks. What issues? Plus, I've got to make sure the condo is ready for them. I thought they'd be here tomorrow. Isn't that what you said?"

"It was, but you're going to love this story. Absalom

gets to Delhi a few days early. He's looking for a beautiful girl to bring with him now that he is away from his mother and her sister wives. Those boys should not be traveling without a guard or secretary, Marco. They just don't know anything about the world. So he finds this beautiful girl, a dancer. She performs in one of the supper clubs in the Chennai District for wealthy men who keep her safe and pay her enough to send home to her parents."

With Harry, I'd learned long ago to just let him talk. Besides, I was driving and had the phone on speaker.

"Okay."

"Absalom convinces her that he will bring her to the United States, where she can learn to surf. Imagine that? Absalom wants to learn how to surf, Marco!"

"It doesn't surprise me."

"He's kept her longer than he was supposed to, and she misses her shift at the supper club, and it causes an uproar. My father himself got angry messages from the Provincial Director, who is a very close confident of the Prime Minister. He calls me in a panic. They're threatening to put Absalom in jail if he doesn't return the girl. So they hire a driver to take them to the airport a day early. They want to tell the airline company they've changed their minds and want to leave now, not wait for the next day. I had to explain to them that wasn't the case, that you don't just tell the pilot to take off because of the other passengers. They've only flown private charter, you see."

"Um, Harry, am I going to hear the punch line today or tomorrow?" I asked.

"Uncle Marco, no worries. I'm almost finished. They show up at the airport and argue with security, and finally, the airline company allows them to purchase a ticket for the girl and re-book their flights to come a day early. But she has no passport, which could be a big problem."

"That's *always* a problem, Harry."

"Don't you know it. She's never had one. Again, accommodations must be made. Both my father and I are calling all the officials we can think of for favors. We get it all worked out, which does delay the plane by nearly an hour. Khalil says the passengers want to lynch them for making them late for their connections, but now they are all set. Just as they board the plane and it begins to take off, the Provincial Director drives out on the tarmac with his cruiser, lights flashing, very dramatic, and tries to shoot the pilots with his pistol."

"Oh God. I hope—"

"No, no. They were fine. The Director was so upset he was shooting all over the place, and airport crews were running for cover. But the plane couldn't stop. I saw it on the news, and it was hilarious. If he hadn't jumped out of the way, they would have run him over."

"Jeez, Harry. Maybe this wasn't such a good idea after all."

"You have no idea what you're in for, Marco. You have to teach them everything."

"I knew that. But no common sense. Is this true?"

"Oh, yes. They are royal people, and royal people don't have to do what the common folk do. Rules are made for the little people, they'll tell you. You better get ready to babysit them twenty-four seven."

"Just what I need." I could see I would have to speak to the sultan, who was also coming over in two weeks, or these boys would be totally out of control.

"In hindsight, we should have brought an escort for them. They're like six-year-old children, Marco."

"What about this girl? We've got to send her back," I stressed.

"Good luck with that. I'm calling you to ask you to get someone to intercede for them when they get to New York. She won't be able to get through customs because of her passport status. Any irregularities, especially now, they'll deport her back to Delhi."

"So she goes back. Simple as that," I said.

"But Absalom can't escort her there, which is what he'll demand, because the Provincial Director will see to it he's locked up. He may never be able to fly into Delhi again. Or out of it, for that matter."

"That's just great. Okay, I better get on the phone with one of my senators. Can you text me the flight number and the arrival time, please?"

"Yes, yes, I will. No problem."

"How long is their layover?"

"This is another problem, Marco. The transfer time is very short, so they may miss their connection. That means getting them a hotel for the night."

"There's one in the airport."

"Yes, I'll set something up just in case. Other than that, things are pretty smooth."

"Uh huh. I better call Senator Campbell to see if we can head off this impending disaster. They have passports, right?"

"Yes, they do."

"How's the Westside Story coming along?"

"Did you tell my father about that? Man was he pissed at me."

"Oh, no. I didn't go there. It didn't come from me."

"He was screaming on the phone. My mother was crying in the background. I couldn't hear a thing, thank goodness. I just handed the phone to her, and they talked it out. I'm never to tell anyone I wrote a gay Westside Story. She had to promise him that she'd burn the manuscript."

"I admit, your family dynamics are a bit out there, Harry. I'd love to talk, but I better get the senator on this."

"Yes, I understand. I'll let you know if they aren't going to make their next connection, Marco."

It took the rest of the way to the office to reach Senator Campbell's aide, and as I arrived in the parking lot, I was still finalizing the details. But at last, I could relax, knowing that even if the girl wouldn't be admitted to the U.S., the princes would be allowed to continue to Tampa. I hoped the senator had his magic gloves on today and wasn't out golfing with the president.

Just in case, I had my pilot ready my jet in Tampa and hold on stand-by.

CHAPTER 9

I DID A short follow-up to the red tide story from yesterday, and this time, Sylvia was with me on the podium, without a live reporter.

"Thank you, Shannon," Sylvia said, with her wide smile, bright white teeth, and blood red lipstick. In the short time she'd been with the station, she'd been very popular, especially with the Cuban population in the greater Tampa area.

"I take it you did not go out for fish last night?" The anchor tilted her head, her eyes flashing, waiting for an answer.

My first instinct was to blush. The question was unexpected.

"Why no," I stuttered, looking down at my script that would be of no use to me now. "I prepared a nice dinner at home. We had steak." I felt my chest go blotchy, my heart racing and my stomach gurgling. My friend Judie would know exactly what I was thinking about. It was impossible to look at the cameraman.

"Come on, Shannon. Look up so we can see that pretty face," the assistant director whispered in my earpiece. His growly voice turned buttery and sexy, which made everything worse. He had a fantastic voice but was not fit for the camera due to his three-hundred-pound size and his pink puffy cheeks.

I obeyed, giving direction to the right, and then noticing the light was on the camera left side, so switched, turning on my stool to give an over-the-shoulder view. I felt ridiculous, but it was what was required of me.

"Atta girl. Perfect. Sylvia? Go top that one."

Sylvia leaned forward with her chin in her hand, something they were repeatedly told not to do, but in this instance, the gesture gave an air of mystery to the set.

"Gee, inquiring minds want to know. What did you and that handsome soon-to-be-husband of yours have for dessert?"

"Back to you, Shannon. Make it sexy."

Caught between the assistant director and my competition, or what was to have been my competition at one time, I flatly refused to play along.

"Custard. Homemade." I stared right into the camera and then gave a slight smirk.

The camera light went out, and Sylvia went on to other news. There was a new art gallery opening in

Tampa, and auditions for the children's ballet company production of Nutcracker were starting next week. Several outdoor concerts were sponsored by various banks and investment firms, most of them Grammy-winning performers who would play a weekend spot and then move on to another town. There were hatchling turtle sightings at the beaches, and volunteers were out combing the low tides to help protect their journey into the ocean and keep the children of locals and tourists from helping themselves to a baby turtle for the drive back home. Residents were asked to keep their patio lights out so as not to confuse them or their mothers who, once they laid their eggs, went back out to sea to welcome them to the family.

I was mesmerized with my good fortune to have found this place after my sister's passing. I remembered the days when our parents took us to Indian Rocks and we built complexes out of sand and buckets and sea water, driftwood, shells, and discarded bird feathers. It suddenly struck me that now, with Marco, I was sort of doing the same. And the ghost of Emily was ever present between us, but as a welcome visitor. At least for me, it was. I hoped that Emily was watching us now and enjoying our adventurous life together as she sat in the back seat. She wouldn't cry, I thought, but she would have a bowl of popcorn.

The set had gone dark when I looked up. Had I

missed the weather portion? Everyone was gone, and the place was deadly silent. I heard monitors playing in the adjoining room where a crowd of station employees were glued to the screen.

Something's happened!

I ran to watch on the screen as half a dozen ambulances and fire rescue vehicles were combing through debris of a collapsed building. I knew before I saw the altered sign hanging from the third floor what it was. The red, white, and blue letters were partly shattered and sparking, swinging by one bolt holding the whole thing in place. It was missing the first letter, and read:

one Frog Development Group.

Sandy was by my side in a flash. "Oh my gosh, Shannon. Is he okay?"

I ran to my desk, looking for my phone, but it wasn't there. I searched the tops of all the other desks, all my drawers, and underneath the desk. I ran back into the set to see if I had left it in the studio but couldn't find it.

"Sandy, where is my phone? Did I leave it in your dressing room?"

"No, I usually check right after I finish, just in case. People leave all kind of things there sometimes when they're nervous. But no. Where is your purse?"

That's when I realized it was no accident my phone

was missing, because my purse was gone as well. The deep bottom drawer in my desk was unlocked with the key still inside the lock, but it was empty.

"I think someone's stolen my purse, Sandy."

Someone from the crowd turned and asked me to be quiet. Jared came up behind me and placed a palm on my shoulder.

"Shannon, the police are looking for you, honey."

I turned and tried to find some sort of hope in his face but was disappointed. His eyes were blinking rapidly. He gripped my shoulder.

"Come into my office. I have Emergency Services on the line there."

"My God, Jared. It can't be Marco."

"I'm afraid it is, Shannon. But I don't know anything more."

One of the college interns turned and announced to the crowd, "They have three dead so far. Not releasing names."

With her clinical tone, I wanted to run up to her and slap her face. But that would be another conversation for a much later time. Holding on to Jared, I made it back to the elevator, and once alone, Jared folded me in his arms.

"Hey, kid. I'm praying for you. For you both."

I got a bit prickly but accepted his comfort anyway. I briefly laid my head against his chest, discovering my knees were shaking. In fact, I was shaking all over.

"You need to sit down," he said as soon as the doors opened. He barely got me to a chair before I collapsed. When I awoke, I remembered him holding me, keeping me from slipping onto the floor. I remembered him shouting for someone to call 9-1-1.

"Thank you, but where is the phone?"

"It's an old-fashioned landline. FCC requirement. Come. I'll help you."

His office was a complete disaster, worse than I'd ever seen it. And he'd been ripping awards and plaques off the wall, tossing them, and missing into a metal garbage can.

"Look, don't pay any attention to any of this. I was having a temper tantrum. Come. Sit here. Here's the phone." He helped me sit in his big brown leather swivel chair and handed me the phone.

"H-hello?"

"Is this Shannon Marr?"

"Yes, it is. Is it Marco?"

"This is Sergeant Ben Healy of the Pinellas County Search and Rescue. There's been an explosion at Bone Frog Development Group building, and we have your fiancé here, getting ready to send him to Bay View Hospital Emergency."

"He's alive?"

"Yes, he is, but he's not conscious. Several members of his staff have been identified as deceased. Can you come down to the hospital?"

"Of course, I'll be right there. Who?"

"We haven't completed the identification. They're all young. All women. But we haven't started the notification process. You can probably help us with the identification."

"Certainly. How bad is he? Where are his injuries?"

"I don't know, ma'am, I'm not a doctor, but he's pretty badly hurt."

"Of course. I'll be right there."

I dropped the phone on the desk, pressed my forearms on a pile of papers, buried my head on top of them, and began to sob.

JARED WAITED WITH me in the Emergency Room, which was on overflow capacity since several other businesses had sustained damage to structures and had injuries as well. I noticed a TMBC camera crew trying to make their way over to me, and Jared pushed them away, screaming. Of course, that was caught on camera and would likely show up somewhere, if not at TMBC itself.

"Assholes."

"They're just doing their job, Jared. The news must go on, even when we're in it. Sucks, but that's the way it is."

"Miss, do you want some water?" a young aide in a light blue uniform asked me.

"That would be heavenly. Thank you."

"I'll have one too," Jared said but was already talking to her backside. "So much for being a big shot."

Slightly relieved that Marco had been confirmed as not critical when I arrived, part of my spirit began to come back. "Relax. I'd be happy to share mine."

"I don't want yours. You're going to need it. What I really need is a drink."

I watched a cluster of family members praying in a circle. A baby was crying, and another ambulance siren could be heard as the whooshing sound of the large automatic doors opened and another gurney was rolled inside with someone grey and lifeless, covered to his neck in a bloody sheet. They were immediately admitted to the surgery wing.

I closed her eyes and asked for healing, white light, strength. I told Emily to help Marco out.

Go rub on his chest, wiggle his toes—he likes that. Tell him he must wake up and that you'll see him eventually, but not now. Please do this for me, Em.

I waited for a reply, with my back straight against the wall for support, my hand entangled in Jared's, resting on my thigh. No one answered. But I kept asking for my sister's help.

I must have fallen asleep, because out of the fog

came the sound, "Mrs. Gambini?"

I opened my eyes and saw that Rebecca was being spoken to by the doctor. Jared was just awakening and jumped to his feet at the same time.

"Hey, I'm Mrs. Gambini. I'm the *new* Mrs. Gambini. She has no business being here." I pointed right at Rebecca, who looked ten years older and very stressed.

"Oh, sweetheart. We both love him, don't we?" Rebecca threw her arms around me, and I pushed her off.

"Get your hands off me. Jared—" I looked around to see if he could help. "Get the police. I want her out of here."

The young Emergency Room doctor was confused. "Just a minute, ladies. I need permission for a procedure. I need the legal spouse of Mr. Marco Gambini."

"Well, it's not her," I blurted out. "Jared, get her out of here. Throw her out if you have to."

Jared was quick to act but a hospital guard, part of the police force, came between them. "Hey, wait a minute, bud. We don't want to cause a scene, and we're delaying the emergency treatment for Mr.—what's his name?"

"Gambini," all four of the arguing parties shouted back.

"Doctor, I'm his fiancé," I said. "We're getting married in the spring. I can prove it, just not here. But I have this," I held up my left hand and demonstrated my huge diamond. Rebecca rolled her eyes.

"She's a little gold digger after my husband's money."

"Ex-husband. You dumped him, remember?"

"Stop it!" the guard called out. "You're divorced, ma'am?"

Rebecca took her time in answering but finally did. "Yes."

"You have any power over his health care?"

"I still have a piece of paper he signed."

"When you were legally married."

"Of course. And I didn't write it. He did."

"You can go, ma'am. Doctor, please proceed." The guard took Rebecca by the elbow and began nearly dragging her out the emergency entrance.

"I'm sorry about all this," I said.

"Now, who's he? If you tell me he's your ex-husband, I'm not going to talk to you either," the doctor said. He was lashing down his patience, but it was about to come unraveled.

"He's my boss and a dear friend."

"Okay, here's the story. We must go in and remove a large piece of metal—we think it was from part of the construction—metal studs or something. It very nearly severed his femoral artery, and if that had happened, well, we wouldn't be having this conversation."

My tongue was stuck to the roof of my mouth. I felt

black circles encroach around both eyes, obscuring more and more of my sight as the seconds ticked by.

"I have to sit down."

"Please." The doctor sat beside me. "He might lose his leg. We may have to take the leg to save his life. He's lost an awful lot of blood. He has a very weakened pulse, and for the time being, he's unconscious, which is the body's way of trying to heal itself. But the damage to that leg is significant. If we cannot get the blood flow back, the leg will atrophy. He has a shattered thigh bone, his knee's screwed up because all his weight came down on his twisted leg from the blast. He was apparently very near where the bomb was planted."

"A bomb? You said a bomb?"

"Yes, ma'am, that's what I'm told, and from the extent of his injuries and the burn marks, well, it's consistent with war injuries I treated in Afghanistan. But I need permission to take the leg. If he doesn't wake up, I may not be able to ask him. I will save his life, one way or the other. But his chances are greatly improved if I don't have to worry about the leg."

"Do what you have to do to save him!" Jared inserted.

The doctor looked at him with full-throttled distain.

"Miss? I need your permission."

I thought about it. I knew what he would choose

for me if the roles were reversed. He'd tell them to save my life and take the leg. But that decision may not be the right one for Marco. As a fighter, he'd want to try. He'd want to be on his feet for the next battle. He was strong and healthy with an enormous will to live, especially if it meant there was some form of retribution coming against the perpetrator of this crime. He certainly wouldn't want to do it from a wheelchair, even though I would love him either way. If he was a complete vegetable, I'd love him.

But I was certain he would not make the same choice for himself he'd make for me. He'd want to first fight to see if his leg could be saved. It didn't matter if he had a limp or if the process was painful or required multiple surgeries. He'd want to remain with both legs, even if one was held together with baling wire and metal rods. He'd find some way to use it as a weapon. He wouldn't even think twice about it.

But there was one problem with that possible solution. If that decision meant that he lost his life, then he'd lose the ability to protect me, and I knew that was his primary goal. And he'd never agree to that.

I inhaled, leaned back, and pressed my spine into the wall, asking for Em's help again. "I can't give you a straight answer." I opened my eyes and investigated the doctor's. "If it costs him his life, then no, take the leg. If that's the only way to save him. If you can save him and not take the leg, even if it's high risk, do not take the leg. I know this man. I know what he'll do to recover. I know the discipline that is such a part of him that will not let him quit. He'd want to make this decision himself, and I'll get flack for making it for him if it comes to that. But if he has a chance to live without taking the leg, then that's the choice I make for him."

The doctor nodded. "You're a very courageous woman. He's going to need that."

"I'm fully on board. Do your best, doctor. This man is still an elite warrior. He is one of those guys who do it all. They are the ones who keep us all safe. You must get him back up on his feet to continue his fight, because he's not done being a warrior. He doesn't want to die off somewhere forgotten, gracefully pass into Heaven. He's going to fight with everything he has left. Don't take away any of his tools. He'll need them. We all need them."

"Very well. Consider it done. I understand the type, ma'am. I saw the tats. Those guys are special, and I haven't lost one yet." He patted my leg and smiled. "I hope you know what a lucky woman you are."

"With every ounce of my being, doctor."

I WAITED TEN hours, sleeping in the waiting room. Finally, they made up a bed for me, and Jared finally went home. Since Marco wasn't in ICU, they allowed me to sleep in his room after his five-hour surgery. The doctor told me there would be many more. He told me Marco should never attempt to jump out of a plane again. We both had a laugh over that one.

But the good news, delivered on a beautiful pink and orange sunlit morning in Tampa, overlooking the blue water and all the little white boats zooming back and forth, the glistening city in the background standing proud, was that he was going to be okay.

"He must have some angel looking after him. For the life of me, I don't understand why that piece of metal didn't completely sever the artery. It was like someone was holding it until we could get in there and see it was going to tear away any second. We got it in time. His blood flow is good already. And he will heal. He won't like the way the leg feels at first. But he'll adapt."

"Thank you, doctor. May I give you a hug?"

"My pleasure."

I returned to Marco's room and climbed in the bed beside him. I looked outside our window at the clouds and the day full of promise and hope. It wasn't a view of the ocean, but it was a wonderful view just the same. If I could stick with the positive, somehow, the evil things coming our way would shed off like an old skin.

I turned on my side, watching his deep rhythmic breathing. His stubble was growing fast. His lips were full and dark pink. His forearms were covered in bands of tats chronicling all that he'd been through—all the men he knew who didn't come home, the people he saved, the ones he couldn't, and the wars he fought. His flesh was like a patchwork quilt stitched together with scars and scratches, holidays here and there where the dark hair didn't grow back at all.

He was like one of the old quilts my grandmother had made, telling stories about the materials she used, the dresses her mother used to wear, all connected with stitches—the sinews of the heart.

I was still the luckiest girl alive.

CHAPTER 10

I AWOKE TO the sounds of snoring nearby and discovered Shannon was asleep in a bed next to me. My head was woozy with a lot of pain coming from my left leg, but the leg itself felt like it had swollen up to the size of a large oblong balloon about to burst. I couldn't wiggle my toes, and I had no feeling on the other side from my waist down.

I tried to raise my head, even to speak, but all I could manage was a small squeak from my throat. I didn't have the strength to try making words or sentences so dropped back into the pillow, exhausted.

My right forearm was taped to a flat plastic brace that looked like a small tray, where a smorgasbord of tubing fed into my system. The insertion of a catheter down below did catch my attention, however, and with very little movement of my right hip, my urethra burned. I howled, which managed to wake Shannon from her slumber.

She sprang to action, hopped off the bed, and gave me a kiss. "How are you doing?" she asked brightly. I could even say she was perky, dammit. I did not feel perky.

"I feel like I've been made into a human punching bag," I mumbled. "This your idea of some sort of sexual domination game? Because I'm not liking it one bit." The pain in my right leg was shooting up the back of my thigh into my butt cheek, where it constricted a muscle there and produced a world-class cramp. "Argh. Oh man, I've got a cramp in the back of my thigh."

"Let me rub it—"

I stopped her from slipping her hand under the covers. Lord knew what she'd find, and the thought of her fingers sliming through my shit made me sick to my stomach. To say I was feeling vulnerable was an understatement.

"Don't touch me!" I wanted it to sound definitive, in control, but I sounded like a scared teenager as my normally deep baritone voice wailed like a wounded female cat in heat.

Her face was filled with tears, but she was smiling.

"Sorry," I mumbled.

"I'm so glad to see you awake, Marco. It was very touch and go. But you have a great doctor. The worst part is over. Now we can concentrate on healing."

"How bad is it? Give it to me straight. I can tell they didn't cut off my dick so whoop-de-doo! Am I going to be one of those guys who sets off all the alarms at the airport screening now?"

"You'll definitely raise attention. But then, you always do get the looks wherever you go, especially if there are ladies nearby."

"I'm not talking about ladies. What did they do to me? Will I be shitting out into a bag from now on? Am I wheelchair-bound?"

"Well, they considered removing your left leg, but I wouldn't let them."

"Atta girl." I was still confused. I closed my eyes to try to remember what had happened and how I got here to the hospital. "What else?"

"You'll have a lot of pins and plates, and a rod or two in your left leg for a time. Not sure about what stays and what gets to come out."

"You put it so delicately, '*Gets to come out!*' Like it is a privilege I get to be wired and plastered back together."

"Your back and neck aren't broken, so no wheelchair at this point."

"What else?" I closed my eyes, tried to adjust my hip again, and stopped, crying out.

"You need me to ask the nurses for something for pain?"

"I don't know. I can't think straight. You tell me. Am I in pain?"

"Sounded like it. Why don't we wait a bit and see if you can begin to feel things? Dr. Patel told me they needed to know what you could move and what caused you pain. Your left leg is the one most damaged. He said you'll have to have more surgeries. All they were able to do was stabilize your broken bones and repair the blood vessels, but your knee is still messed up and will have to be replaced."

"Ouch, not looking forward to that."

"I was told to push the call button when you awoke. Let's do that now." She leaned over, took the small device no bigger than a Vienna sausage, and pushed a white button on the end of it.

"I could have done that, Shannon."

"But I nicely did it for you, Marco. Say 'thank you, Shannon.'"

"Thank you, Shannon."

The loudspeaker above my bed squawked unintelligibly, but Shannon answered, "He's awake, and I think he needs something for pain."

The speaker cracked and then shut off. About five minutes later, a young pretty nurse entered the room with a vial and a needle.

"So where are you having pain, Mr. Gambini?"

I pointed with my forehead to the middle of my

groin. "I'm not joking. My dick hurts, at least I think it's my dick." I adjusted my hip again and the hot searing pain returned twice as strong as the first time.

"I'm sorry, Mr. Gambini. I'll give you a little something, but that's from the catheter in your penis."

"What did they do, fuckin' put it in sideways?"

Shannon covered her mouth, snickering.

"I'm going to look and see if it's infected. Sometimes they do these pretty quickly and they can scrape the insides."

When the nurse lifted the covers, Shannon looked away. I tried to raise myself up to examine the pulsing body part, but it was no use.

"Oh, I can see it now. Looks like there is a little blood, and some bruising. I can place some numbing cream there, which will help. You're already on a whole regimen of antibiotics, so that's not necessary, but you're going to have to live with this for a few days. They'll take it out as soon as they can, and that means we're getting you up to use the toilet. But until then, I'm afraid we're leaving this in and monitoring the output. Don't expect a miracle."

I laid back, staring at the ceiling while the nurse left then returned with a small jar of salve, which she applied around the opening where my penis accepted the plastic tubing. She followed the path of the tube where it was depositing urine into a small jar on the floor.

"Your color looks good, and you're peeing up a storm, so I'd say, compared to how you could have looked, you're doing very well."

"Gee thanks. When do I get to eat?"

"Going to be just jello and broth for lunch and dinner. I'm sorry we can't offer you the gourmet menu, but you'll get there soon. Not to worry."

"They said if I wanted to, I could take a shower," Shannon asked the nurse. "I've been up all night in the ER, and I feel dirty."

"Yes, you can use the guest shower at the end of the hall. I'll get you some scrubs and a towel. You need shampoo?"

"Yes, please," answered Shannon.

After the nurse left, I saw her eyes were red and puffy. Little flashes of activity popped up in my brain, and I began to remember things slowly.

"This happened at Bone Frog Development, right?" I asked her.

"Yes. They said it was a bomb."

"I didn't see any bomb. But I do remember looking out the window when something hit me from the side—my left side. It felt like someone slapped my left hip with a spiked baseball bat, and I lost my footing. I smelled sulfur, and I almost puked."

Then I remembered I was talking to two new hires

Celia was introducing to me, and as she was talking, her chest erupted when a piece of metal stud nearly cut her in half.

"Celia, the gal from HR. She was badly injured," I said. "I saw it. How bad?"

"There are four fatalities. She was one of them," Shannon told him. "I'm so sorry, Marco."

I couldn't get the vision of the explosion out of my head. "I couldn't move. I tried, and then I just passed out."

Suddenly, I remembered Harry and the arrangements for the two princes to arrive in Tampa. I attempted to get up as if I was going to change my clothes and drive myself to the office. But immediately, my limitations sent me back into the mattress and pillow. "Did Harry get the two boys to Tampa?"

"Yes. Rhea told me to tell you they're arriving—" she checked her watch. "No, I think they should be here now. Apparently, there was something that held them up in New York. She said to tell you Pete and Ron picked them up in the jet and are bringing them to the condo. They know about the bomb, and so does the sultan."

"Okay. I'm sure Rhea and the crew will watch over those boys."

"She said to tell you, 'Like glue' so you needn't worry."

"Who else?"

"Jennifer, Connie, and Maggie. I only remember meeting Jennifer. I think the other two were new interns or new hires getting their paperwork straightened out. Those were the pictures of people they said were killed. I'm so sorry, Marco."

I was getting sleepy, probably from the drug the nurse had injected into my tubing. Just then, she arrived with a folded towel and some blue-grey hospital sweats, along with a plastic bag filled with personal items for Shannon's shower.

"Here you go. Be quick about it because I believe Dr. Patel is going to stop by very soon." Shannon took the pile and promised me she'd be right back.

"So how bad is it?" I asked the nurse, hoping to get more technical information about my condition.

"I haven't seen Dr. Patel's work on you, but apparently, they came close to removing your left leg. You have pins holding everything together until some of the soft tissue heals."

"Shannon said they still have to repair my knee?"

"You're going to be in and out of here quite a bit, yes."

"Any other damage elsewhere?"

"I don't think so from your chart. But he'll go over that with you, Mr. Gambini. You're very lucky he was on call yesterday. You got one of the best orthopedic surgeons in Florida."

"That's where we are! Finally, someone tells me."

"Where did you think you were?"

I shrugged.

"All this happened at your office. You should see that building."

"I can only imagine. Will I be able to walk soon?"

"Finally, something I know. They might have you up tonight. Depends on whether he lets you out of bed to put any weight bearing on this leg, but I highly doubt it. I think they'll have to do the knee fairly soon."

"How many injured?"

"The news is reporting twenty-three injured with four fatalities."

"I guess it was a big deal then. Where are the police?"

"Right outside your door. They want to talk to you when you feel up to it. You should get it over with as soon as you're able."

"Why spoil the party? Send them in."

The nurse next shuttled the pair of investigators into my room and asked if they needed her to stay.

"No, ma'am. We'll keep it short."

"Please do. His fiancé is showering down the hall and his doctor is due in to speak to him. I'm going to do my best to make sure he has a long, restful night's asleep as much as possible. You can come back tomorrow if you have more questions, understood?"

"Yes, ma'am," the younger of the two investigators answered. The two of them stood on either side of the bed, studying my face, and following a bulge under the covers where all the action was.

"Mr. Gambini, did you have any warning this was about to occur? Did anyone threaten you or make disparaging comments to your face or anyone else on the team, that you know of?"

"It was my ex-wife, Rebecca Gambini. She's the one behind this. She practically told me so."

"Um, we met with her downstairs, and she definitely appeared to be most distraught. She appeared to us to look like a woman in pain, that she cares that you were caught up in it," said the younger investigator.

"Still, I think she's responsible. She might not have wanted to hurt me, but I'm sure she's at least partially responsible for the bomb that injured and killed others."

"How did you know it was a bomb, sir?"

"Because everyone's been talking about it. And I felt some sort of impact, something big hit me."

"Explain why you think Rebecca is behind this attack."

"She made a comment about my first fiancé, who just happens to be Shannon's sister. Emily died in an auto accident fifteen years ago. We had a heated discussion regarding the Trident Towers, which she wants to be part of, and she has no right. But she won't leave me alone. At the end, she asked me if I thought lightning could strike twice."

"And you took this to mean, what? That you could lose your new fiancé, or that she might have had something to do with your first one?"

I noticed Shannon standing in the doorway, her palm covering her mouth. I knew it was a mistake that she'd heard the investigator's question. It was the one detail I'd left out of my discussion with Shannon, and I knew this was going to be a huge problem for her. The look that I shared with her in that long moment broke my heart. Her expression was the same as if she'd walked in on me in bed with another woman. I could tell she felt betrayed.

And in fact, she was. I hadn't been completely honest with her. Now I was about to pay the price for it.

I called out to her, but she quickly disappeared.

"Shit." I muttered under my breath. "You have to help me protect her, officers. I didn't tell her about the veiled threat and—"

"Sounded pretty overt to me," said the younger investigator.

"What I mean is that she may have been the intended target. The blast or whatever it was that hit me like a ton of bricks came from her office. You need to keep her away from Rebecca. I don't have any of my security detail around me. You've got to help me get her some protection."

The two men shared a quick glance and then excused themselves.

I punched the button again. When the radio squawked, I screamed, "Get in here and get me a goddamned telephone!"

CHAPTER 11

I GRABBED MY extra gym bag stuffing my clothes inside the large satchel and flew to the elevator. I pushed the button down from the 4th floor surgery center to the lobby. I was still stuffing the remainder of my dress I'd worn this morning into my bag, not watching where I was going, when I ran into Rebecca Gambini.

"Oh my God, I'm so glad I found you. Listen, you're not safe," Rebecca whispered. Her disheveled look did alarm me. She was normally so put together, but right now, her hair was tied in a knot and held with, of all things, a clip—something I never thought I'd see her wear. Her eye makeup was streaked. Lipstick had worn out hours ago. A mustache of perspiration had formed on her upper lip.

I jumped back as Marco's ex tried to grab me. "Don't you dare touch me. I'll scream. I'll have you arrested. You know, Marco has already told the police investigators you're the cause of the whole bombing. You killed innocent people, Rebecca. A small child was injured and twenty others hurt, some seriously. Have you no shame, no conscience?"

It felt good to let it all out full tilt. My hours of waiting and then carefully stepping on eggshells while Marco awakened and took stock of what had happened had only built up the pressure to act, to strike out, to right the wrong done by the bomb and by the betrayal of my own fiancé with information about my sister's death and the possible involvement *with his ex-wife!*

Rebecca came after me, pulling on my top and grabbing the bag's handle. I called out to the guards at the hospital entrance. "Help! This woman is trying to steal my purse!"

Both uniformed officers, a man, and a woman, ran to me immediately, the woman speaking into a shoulder mic, asking for backup. Two bystanders, both hospital staffers, came to my aid, and the group of them held Rebecca back while I flew through the automatic glass doors of the front of the building and out into the freedom of the street.

But, without a purse, without a cell phone, I was completely stuck with no means of transportation, no way to call to anyone for help. I cursed myself for not thinking about all this while I was sleeping next to Marco, waiting for him to open his eyes. I wasn't ready.

I should have been five steps ahead of all that, because now I had to act with only scant tools to fight the fight.

A cab pulled up and asked me if I needed a ride.

"I'm so sorry, but my purse has been stolen in the bomb blast," I lied, "and I was just trying to get home to get some things before I come back to be with my friend."

"How far do you live?"

"I'm on the island."

"Ah, never mind. I'll take you there. Come on, get in."

"Thank you so much. You don't know how much this means to me."

"Hey, if that had happened to me, I'd be doing the same thing. You gotta come first for your friends and family. You worry about who the thief is later. He'll get his due."

I watched the scenery flash by and noticed how gaunt and unhealthy I looked in the glass reflection. "He sure will," I whispered back, thinking about Marco.

"So where are we going, Miss?" the cab driver asked, stopping behind a line of cars, holding his hands off the steering wheel. "I'm pretty handy with a hammer, but I'm not a mind reader."

I smiled. "I'm so sorry. I'm not myself. It's in Indian Rocks Beach, 2245 Beach Trail. Near the Kooky

Coconut."

"I know right where that is. My kids love it there. They love the ice cream better than the beach. We'll give you a flat rate, forty bucks. If you can find some cash, good. If not, well, do a favor for someone else some day in return. Are we square?"

"Yes, thank you. I think I might have money in my other purse. Not sure, but if you give me your name and address, I'll mail you a generous check. Thanks again, so much."

"No problem." He drove for five minutes, glanced back at me in the rearview mirror, and then again, several times later. "Hey, you're that weathergirl, Shannon Marr. Isn't that right?"

"Yes, yes, that's me."

"You got a rich boyfriend. Is he the one who is at the hospital?"

Now I didn't know what to do. Our relationship was all over the Tampa area, since the proposal was even done on-air. I'd interviewed him, done stories about the Trident Towers. There was no skulking around Tampa without being recognized. So how should I answer that question? If I started telling too many lies, my credibility would go right out the window. But at the present time, I didn't know who my ally was and who were the people who had deceived me.

"He is. They're going to prep him for further surgery. He was badly banged up. I'm supposed to get him some papers at the house and bring them down to the hospital. I totally spaced out that I didn't have a car, no purse, wallet, no cell phone, and the clothes the hospital gave me."

He cackled, throwing his head back. "Well, no worries there. You make any pair of scrubs look good, Shannon. Don't you worry your little head about it. Uncle Andy's going to get you home, and I'll take you right back to the hospital afterward. I can't wait to tell the missus and the kids that I took Shannon Marr on an errand, twice in one day!"

I smiled and tried to play along but needed to be alone. I needed time to think. The last place I needed to be back at the hospital with the nurses, the investigators, and Rebecca! Hopefully, they had her under control by now. I remembered Marco's expression when he saw me standing in the doorway while he told them Rebecca had confessed to being involved in Emily's death.

How could he hide that from me? Emily was the most important person in my life before she met Marco, and with his betrayal, despite my feelings for him I couldn't deny, my trust had been broken. I wondered how he could think that kind of stab in the back would be okay with me.

"I appreciate your kindness, but I'm going to quickly go through things, and then I'll call some people from his office to help me find what I need if I can't locate them. So, thank you, but I think I'm covered for the return."

"Okay, we'll be there in about ten then."

I thanked him profusely again.

Rather than reveal which house we lived in, I had him drop me off at the root of the access trail to the beach. "The driveway is non-existent, and I don't want you scraping the car in the alleyway made for scooters."

As he pulled to a stop, he handed me his card. "Please, Shannon, it's been a pleasure, and if you ever need a good driver—you know I drive limos too. I'm your guy. My P.O. Box is on the back, and my personal cell I never give out except to good clients. Give me a try, and if you never send the check, it's just been a pleasure to help you out."

"Thanks so much," I looked at the card. "Andy. How much is the fare?"

"Like I said, forty bucks flat rate. You send it when you can, but it's been nice meeting you!"

He sped off as I ran in the opposite direction to my house then hit the beach, doubling back, climbing up on the access bridge and then walking up one block to my bungalow. I picked up the key under the doormat, another thing I was going to change, and let myself inside, locking the door behind me.

I'd hardly had time to get my breath when I heard a banging on the door. It made me jump. I slipped into the bedroom and peeked through the corner of the drapes on the window perpendicular to the front door. My car was right behind the man in a mechanics jumpsuit.

So now I'd have wheels! Opening the door, I stared at his face.

"Geez, what's the matter with you?" he asked.

"The bombing—Marco's in the hospital."

"Oh, that was his office? I'm so sorry. How bad is he?"

"Major broken leg, knee's banged up. But at least he's alive. Four others didn't make it out."

"Was it a gas leak?"

"No, it was a bomb."

"Yeah, I had intuition about that. You know, your car was tampered with. First, they disconnected the battery on one side, but they punched holes in one of your hoses, and your engine would have overheated if you'd gotten it to start. Now you're talk about this bombing, and to me, and I'm no cop, but it looks like someone didn't want you to go anywhere."

"Or wanted Marco to drive me. I think that was the goal."

"Well, you guys have enough on your plate. But I'll send the bill by email, and Marco can take care of it when he's out of the hospital. In the meantime, you be careful. Watch for little things because even though I went through the car, looking for other stuff—checked the tires, made sure nothing was put in the water or drained the coolant, gas tank, etc., you never know. No driving at night alone in case something I didn't catch pops up, okay?"

"That's fair."

"Here are your keys," he handed them over. I could have hugged him I was so happy to have wheels. As he was turning away, I called out to him.

"In the commotion with the explosion, somehow, I lost my purse and phone. Where can I get one of those 'temporary' ones, cheap?"

"Any of the liquor stores would have burner phones for sale. Some of the stereo stores too. Walmart has some with instant prepaid service. There's a Walmart just down the road about two miles. Big one too."

"Thanks so much." I hesitated but decided to ask another question of the friendly mechanic. "By the way, do you work on anyone else's cars at Marco's company?"

"You mean on his dime?"

"Yes."

"Well, he's got a truck for Rhea or maybe Dax. Not sure who drives it the most. Company truck."

I nodded.

"He's got the delivery van for hauling things to and from here and the airports, picking up supplies, things they need. And then there's Rebecca's Mercedes. He still services it."

"How long has that been going on?"

"Oh hell, they first came out here in, well, it would be about seven or eight years ago. She lives in Manhattan, of course, but when she drives it down, it always needs servicing, detailing, and little things fixed."

"That never changed after the divorce?"

"Well, he kept paying the bill. So I guess nothing changed, did it? At first, I wondered, about a year ago when I did some work for her, when the divorce had been finalized, and I figured he'd object if he didn't intend on paying for it, and he didn't squawk at all. Pays in full and quick. Wish I had a hundred customers just like him."

After the mechanic left, I went in search of any cash I'd left in a purse or favorite jacket or drawer, finding only a few bills and some coins. I searched Marco's things and then pawed through his little secret drawer by the bed where he kept his special creams and lubes—his little surprises for me in bed. But despite some interesting toys he'd yet to show me, there was no evidence of a second secret life he might be living outside our relationship, and there certainly was no cash there, either. But on the top of our dresser, I'd forgotten about a bowl that contained spare change he'd deposit there before taking his evening shower. I picked out all the quarters and even a couple silver dollars, which added up to nearly twenty-five dollars. I hoped it was enough to buy a phone.

I placed the coins in a baggie and drove to the local drug store, finding a prepaid phone on special for just under fifteen dollars, and after tax, I had a few quarters to spare. The packaging touted that it would accept collect calls but no messages, which was perfect. The young man behind the counter inserted the activation chip and turned the phone on to make sure it worked, handing it back to me with a few simple instructions for use.

Sitting in the parking lot outside, I dialed Judie but got no answer. Then I dialed Jared, almost hanging up before he answered.

"Jared Newsome."

"Jared. It's Shannon. Listen, I'm in some trouble."

"Already? I just left you—what?—a few hours ago at the hospital. How's Marco and how the heck did you manage to get into trouble at a hospital?"

"Marco did well in surgery, but it's going to be a long road for him. Remember when last night I couldn't find my purse and cell phone?"

"Yeah. From the look of this number, my guess is you bought another?"

"Yes. Just got it. Still haven't found my purse, which I think was deliberately taken with all my contacts in that phone."

"Okay, so where's the trouble part and why are you so stressed and buying phones? I figured I would have heard it on the news if he—anyway, what the heck's going on?"

"I overheard a conversation I wasn't supposed to hear. He admitted to the investigators Rebecca might have been responsible for my older sister's death. He told them Rebecca was probably the bomb procurer, the one who set it up. Everyone in the world wants to talk to me, and I need to disappear somewhere. Marco even told me I'm not safe. I don't feel safe, even with all the bodyguards he's proposing. I don't know who to believe anymore and who I can trust."

"I'm honored you called me."

"Don't get any ideas."

"One can hope."

"There is no hope, Jared. But I need your help."

"Why don't you feel you can trust Marco?"

"Because he lied to me. Or he omitted this information. Why would he do that, Jared?"

"Well, he did just wake up in a hospital with injuries from a bombing. Maybe he didn't have time. Are you sure you're thinking clearly?"

"That's why I need to get away. I need somewhere I can think, piece things together."

"Where are you calling from?"

"I'm outside the drug store where I bought the phone. But I don't have any credit cards or money right now. I can go to the bank tomorrow and get all that straightened out, but could you spot me a few hundred dollars just for a couple of days so I can buy gas and food, a motel room—whatever I need, until I figure out what's going on?"

"I could go by the ATM, pick up some cash for you, but not too much, you know. I have a limit."

"Yes, I do too. Could you bring it by—wait, even better, can we meet at the Crab Shack? I'm not sure it's safe at home."

"Why not meet here at my office?"

"No, even worse. Too many people asking questions. I need time to do some research."

"You're welcome to stay with me. You'd be safe there. No one would bother you."

"That's a bad idea. Listen, if you can help me out, I'll really owe you one. Big exclusive, breaking news type event I'll give you when I got it. Okay?"

"What are you working on?"

"I don't think I should talk about it."

"Okay, then don't promise something you can't deliver, Shannon. I'm just happy to help, although I have a bone to pick with your boyfriend for putting you in this situation. Rather inconvenient him being in the hospital and all."

"Funny. He told the investigators he thought I was the target, not him."

"And how did he come to that?"

"Because the bomb was planted in my office, next to his. If I'd been there, I'd be dead, Jared."

"Now this is the part where you tell me you're so grateful to have a job, that I saved your life today, and waited with you until I couldn't see straight while he was in surgery that you've reconsidered your leaving, because you discovered he's lying to you and you've suddenly gotten the urge to become an investigative reporter and will give up traveling all over the world in private jets. Please tell me you were going to say all that."

"Hardly. Just come. We'll sort it all out later. For right now, I need funds, and I need to disappear. And I promise, with your help, I'm going to research this whole thing and Rebecca's involvement in Emily's accident. I want you to bring all the files you can find on it, the interview notes, police reports, everything. I want to know what happened to the guy who got the DUI."

"Whoa, whoa! All that happened in California, Shannon. How do I get those records?"

"You do someone a favor. Cold case. Bombshell exclusive you'll share. You must have some contacts in the San Francisco Bay area you can lean on."

"Where was the accident?"

"Up in Sonoma County. The girls were supposedly up for a weekend in wine country."

"So, name some towns, Shannon."

"Santa Rosa, Petaluma. Sonoma—Sebastopol."

"Sebastopol! That's it. I had a buddy in college who inherited his parents apple farm, and he later became a cop. I think he was chief of police in Sebastopol for a spell. I'll try to look him up."

"And you'll need newspaper contacts."

"Kind of discouraging there. We don't really share. But give a cop a chance to solve a cold case or right a wrong, he's all over it. I'll bring over what I can find right away, and then I'll do more later. And not a word of this to anyone, Shannon. You're not to tell the police, Marco, no one. I gotta protect my sources, and I won't give them up. I don't want to get an old friend in trouble."

"I understand. And you're helping a newer friend stay out of trouble. I need to know why Marco would hide all this from me. Don't give me any names. I want to see the records. We could say someone wanted justice and left the files in the mailbox for you."

"It happens. Not to me, but it happens."

"Jared, we have to be careful. If the wrong person went to prison over this, if it was someone else's order, that makes it murder, not manslaughter. It's a whole new ball game. That's why I'm going to have to disappear for a bit. I'm going to need your help on that."

"Well, hell's bells, I may be the Program Director, but I can do a quick Witness Protection caper at the drop of a hat. I'm flexible, good looking, willing to save your life, and I adore you. Explain to me why you want this guy, who's practically old enough to be your father? The guy who doesn't tell you the truth?"

I inhaled, reset my nerves, closed my eyes, and thought about everything for a minute, and then I said, "Because, in spite of everything, I love him."

CHAPTER 12

I WAS ON the telephone when Dr. Patel came in to see me. I motioned that I was almost done with my call. Without expression, the doctor waited nearly a minute before checking his watch again and then forcibly removed the phone from my hand, turning it off, and placing it in the large pocket of his lab coat.

"I was just finishing up, as I showed you," I said defensively.

Dr. Patel cut me off. "You don't get to do that. This is my hospital. You don't work for me. You hired me to do a job, and I'm going to do it, or I will send you someplace else where they don't care what kind of quality care you get. Am I making myself perfectly understood, Mr. Gambini?"

"Yes. Are you going to give me my phone back? I have important—"

"Oh, we are so important. I understand you have yet to thank the woman who saved your leg."

"I thought you did that."

"No, Mr. Gambini, I'm talking about the woman who made the decision that I should take your balls rather than take your leg."

"What?" I was ready to throw myself at Patel.

"You need to listen to me carefully, Mr. Gambini. We have a few more things left to do. Or, if you like, I can stop doing anything, and then we can watch you heal into a cripple. It will be funny to see this former, big strong man hobbling around, chasing women, and pushing people around with his cane. People will laugh at him, and they should. Because he's a very, very stupid man who has an enormous ego and hasn't yet learned his lesson."

"What lesson?" I asked.

"First, we crawl. Then we walk. Then we run. Do you ever remember hearing that during your SEALs training? Do you know that there are people who break records and win marathons who crawl or walk during part of the race? Figure that one out. Do you know why that is?"

"Because that's how they've trained."

"No, Mr. Gambini. It's because they are not idiots. They are true champions. They do what they can do, but they do *all* they can do. They put their whole heart into it, to the last drop of their blood. Those people are winners. You used to be a winner when you were a

SEAL—"

"When called, I could be again," I interrupted.

"I don't think so. You're going to look like Mr. Toad walking down the road because your ego is so attached to that cauliflower next to your ear you call a cell phone that you're not paying attention to getting your body ready to be able to be all you can be. If you don't pay attention to it, it will in turn kick you in the ass."

"You have a crappy bedside manner, doctor."

"I have a horse's ass for a patient. You might think you're special with your millions, your tats, and the fun things you get to do. Meanwhile, I'm fixing people's frames so their plumbing works, so their head doesn't roll to one side. I'm a simple car mechanic. And you want to take that car out and run it on three wheels, telling yourself you're the best driver on the planet. But you can't win any races with three wheels. And your mechanic is screaming to you to let him fix the tire. But of course, you have much more important things going on. World-class things. Have you ever wondered why someone might want to blow up this wonderful body of yours? Think about it. Someone may want you dead, Mr. Gambini."

Dr. Patel started to walk out when I said, "I'm sorry. You're right. I've been a jerk."

"That's not the word I would have used. I understand that you let that woman walk out of here who stayed with you all night long so she could see you first thing when you woke up, who slept in a damned plastic chair in the waiting area for six hours, hoping for some good news that I might bring her. She told me to take the risk, save the leg, and—hopefully—also save your life. She had courage. And yet, you let her just walk away from this place without even a 'thank you.' What kind of a man are you? A big man or a little scared one?"

"I'm better than that. I had reasons for not telling her everything I knew. I just found out. I was trying to keep her from danger."

"That's between the two of you. But remember what I said in the beginning. This is my hospital, not your office. We do things my way here, not your way. Here, we respect people not for who they are but for what they can do. Right now, all you can do is get well. That's it."

"But I have to find her. And I must find out about her older sister's accident, because it might not have been an accident."

"Well, have it your way, Mr. Gambini. It will certainly be no accident when your big toe rubs flush against the arch in your other foot. When you pee and shit out of the same hole. When getting up to put your underwear on is so painful you have to go back to bed for an hour. These things could happen. Do I have your attention now?"

"You do. And I apologize."

"Okay." Dr. Patel sat on the edge of the bed, leaning into me. "I am going to need to operate tomorrow on that left knee. I was worried about your hip, since the full force of your body landed on that leg, and it apparently was bent back at a very unnatural angle. Hips come before knees. Since the hip checks out fine, now we can focus on the knee."

"How long will I be here, then, recuperating?"

"If your femur is beginning to heal and accepts the pins and rods we've placed there to stabilize it and the knee operation goes as planned, you'll be out in two, maybe three days."

"What about this damned catheter?"

"I might just keep that in for spite, Mr. Gambini."

I didn't detect any change in the doctor's expression. He looked deadly serious.

"That's not funny."

"We can remove it when you can go pee in a toilet, even if you have to have help doing so. Once that begins, then we no longer need the catheter. Until then, we advise against wetting the bed. Patients who do so have to mop the hallway afterwards and frequently get spanked with a stiff boar bristle hairbrush."

The doctor was funny as hell but at my expense. I

had to convince him that there was danger all around him, and that if Shannon was on her own, her life was in jeopardy.

"Allow me to assemble my team for a meeting, a brief meeting. We'll put into motion a plan, and we will stick to the plan. But I must lead them. That's the way it works in my world. Someone in my group has been compromised, and until I find out who, everyone is suspect and no one is safe, least of all Shannon. And time is of the essence."

Dr. Patel stood. "I will return your phone provided you limit your calls to one hour a day."

"But that's not nearly enough—"

"Is this your hospital, Mr. Gambini?"

"No, but—"

"And you will be allowed one meeting, today if you prefer. Tomorrow is surgery day, so no meetings. You must get a good night's sleep. Your minions can serve you very well, I suspect, if you let them. Your job is to let your body heal. Stress, especially undue stress, emotional agitation, is not your friend. I personally think they dissolve stitches."

"But I can work, right? I can text and give directions, and I can send emails from my phone."

"Yes, I believe so."

"Then I'll be the model patient. You won't have to worry about me."

"Remember what I said to you initially. This is my hospital. It's not going to be transformed into your office." Before he left the room, he turned, reached into his pocket, and tossed me my cell.

"Thanks, Doc. When will I see you next?" I asked.

"I'll stop by tonight between eight and ten, depending. I'm going to make sure my assessment still holds, so don't do anything stupid like try to walk or fall out of bed. We had a Pacific Islander family here one time visiting, and our guy was a huge man. I think he topped three-fifty. Naturally, he had to have both knees done at once because, well—"

"He is a lineage from a warrior class."

"Exactly. I mean, my cousins are still digging archeological sites, brewing chai, and doing telemarketing on their stationary bicycles generating electricity for his home—you know that little Indian guy who always calls you with the name of Chad or Kevin to tell you your car or computer is nearly out of warranty? I'm probably related to him."

"Don't beat yourself up. My great grandfather made a small fortune selling wine to Garibaldi during the great unification war."

"I'm not familiar with that one."

"Half Italian," I said pointing to my chest. "It's a different kind of bravado, but wine can be very important to a successful campaign."

"Oh, indeed. I agree with you there. Well, despite me telling him to wait for the orderlies to take him to the toilet, he had several of his family members help him go, and of course, he fell. So that night, I didn't get any sleep. I had to replace his hip, which was now fractured, and then we went in a couple of days later and re-did the knee that I'd done so well the first time."

"Did he stay down?"

"I hated to do it, but it was a necessity. Told the family they'd be arrested if they tried it again, and we tied the poor fellow to the bed. He's back out there playing Rugby again. I'm sure our paths will cross another time or two."

"That's a great story. The moral is do not slip in the bathroom."

"No, don't get your friends to try to take you there. First, you have a catheter, and I can make it so you are constantly reminded of it, Marco, so don't test me. But second, your femur is weaker than an eighty-year-old woman's right now. I'm not sure I can put it all back together again. It's a very bad idea, Marco. Be patient. Like I said, let your minions do the work for you. Have your meeting, but try to be done by eight or I'll embarrass you in front of them."

"You remind me of a couple of my drill instructors at Coronado, Dr. Patel. I think you might have missed your calling."

"No, I'll let the Navy train them. I'll let their wives and girlfriends love the hair off their bodies, and I'll patch them up when I can. I know my place in the world, Mr. Gambini. I'm not going to try to be anything I'm not. But I know a thing or two about people. I know when I meet a hero. And I know when I see the woman he should go after. If you don't get her back, it will be the worst decision you will ever make in your life."

"Coming from experience?"

"That information is private. I'm a happily married man with two small children. My life is just as exciting as I want it to be. I go to sleep at night knowing I've made the world a better place."

"So do I, doctor. So do I."

I was sorry to see him go. But I was getting texts already from my team with information on Shannon and other things concerning the bombing. I hoped I had time to talk to the doctor at length about his life, what he'd lived through, and how he came to be such an incredible human being.

I stuffed the room with nearly twenty people. I was grateful, even though there were a couple of them with patches and splints, that everyone who could come did. For most, it was the first time they'd been in contact with each other.

"First, we want to remember our teammates who

did not survive. Jennifer, Connie, Celia, and Maggie. Celia was doing a great job with the new hires, and many of you have your jobs because of her."

Someone sniffled. Half the group watched me, and the other half looked down, fidgeting with their shoes.

"Nobody comes to work and expects to die. Unfortunately, I've seen too much of it. It's especially heinous when innocents are caught in the fray. Death is indiscriminate, can happen at any time, and it devastates those who are left behind. What I'm asking of you, and you're all civilians, is that you reach inside your heart and make what you do from now on count. Let's find out what happened and make sure we can bring them to justice. Nobody is to go streaking out on their own. We're a team. Lone wolfs die in the wild. The ones who survive stay with the pack, blend in, and find a place there. It's a crazy, fucked up world out there. But we're in this together. We're building a project I've wanted to do since I first got out of service. I bought the property on an option before I had any idea how I was going to pay for it. But we're the kid who throws his hat over the fence, which means that now somehow, he must get over that fence or his mother will kill him if he comes home without his only hat. He tosses it because it kills off his options."

I tried to make eye contact with every person in the room. I knew some would have to let the events percolate before they could come out of their shell. For others, it would spur them to action. Many, it would add to their fear of living every day. Some would help others on the team deal with it. Others would become the comic relief, and even make fun of the leadership from time to time. They were a ragtag squad of mostly kids who could have made more money packing books at Amazon, but they were there to help me bring my idea into fruition. They were one unit. One powerful force for good.

"I'm proud of you all. Hang in there. It's not going to be easy, but we're going to get this project built, and we're going to bring the evil to justice. We rely on each other, help each other, hold up each other, just like we did on the Teams. This isn't just one of those incidents that will languish on for years and no one ever finds out what or why it happened."

I sat back because my back was hurting me now. I reached for a pair of readers I'd had brought up from the hospital store and read over some notes I'd made.

"We're going to replace those we've lost. I need a good HR person, and I need them pronto."

"I got that covered, Boss. We know a lady who is out of work because her contractor retired. She's terrific. I've tried to hire her for years."

"Okay, you and Dax go after her. Offer her what's a little above good. And, by the way, all of you get a ten percent raise for staying on board. If you must leave, go with my blessing. Anyone in that category?"

I looked over the little crowd, and nobody raised a hand.

"Okay, that's taken care of. Rhea, did you find out anything about this boyfriend of Rebecca's?"

"Working on it, Boss. He's all bark, no bite. Knows zip about construction. She got to someone on the Planning Commission. I'm heading that one off at the pass."

"Are we going to have to go through a third re-design?"

"Not if you can get your senator to help out."

"I'll call him next." I checked off a couple of items and crossed out something I changed my mind on.

"Karin, I need you to see if there is any chatter in the sultan's orbit. Reach out to him and reassure him that we have support in Washington and that his sons will be safe on my life."

"Absolutely. I also am putting out feelers to see how deep Rebecca, or whomever is responsible for this, got, whether there is a faction that is resistant to the project for some reason."

"Excellent idea."

"Kevin, you're on surveillance. Any idea where Shannon went off to?"

"She's not at your house, Boss. I asked at the station, but everyone is in limbo, scattered and covering stories, helping affiliates get information. But Jared left early, about four o'clock. He usually waits until the ten o'clock news is over before he leaves. No one seems to know where he is, so I'm guessing she might have reached out to him."

"I think that's a good assumption. Keep working on that. She has a friend named Judie who works there too. See what she has to say, or see if she's perhaps covering something up, lying."

"There's also some tension with Shannon and this Bunny evening anchor person. But she doesn't look the type."

"Hard to see Dolly Parton become a Unabomber," said Dax.

Everyone laughed.

"Find Judie. Find Jared too."

"Art, you're former FBI. What are they looking at now? And do we know where Rebecca is?"

Art had been standing in the back row and made his way up front. "She was going to be detained, but she got that Criminal Defense attorney, Hernandez, who got her released. He's agreed to bring her in for questioning tomorrow."

He stumbled on his words a bit, then stopped, and scratched his head.

"What's going on, Art?"

"Well, in my line of work, you get a pretty good read on people very quickly. And I'm not feeling it for Rebecca. I just don't get that she'd want to murder innocent people. I don't see the bomb as being her idea. I just don't see how she would get access to a pro like the person who planted it. If I may say so myself, I think you should have Forest look into it. I think that bomber had military background, from the placement of the bomb to making one strong enough to collapse the building but not blow up everyone. That takes skill."

"I thought the same thing," said Forest. "To me, it looked like you and Shannon, or maybe just Shannon, was the target."

I added my opinion. "Because I wasn't killed, I'm thinking I wasn't the target. That's why it pointed me to Rebecca. She hates Shannon, she clearly is angry, but in our private conversation, she practically begged me to come back."

"You want me and Art to work together, go over what the police have as far as evidence?" asked Forest. "I think both of us have some skills in getting some things out that aren't released to the public."

"Yes. Excellent. And see if you can get a freelance profiler. We need a read on who Rebecca has been spending time with. Maybe she's being coerced."

I went over other job assignments, putting people

in charge of finding another location to set up the offices. A team volunteered to help with cleanup after the police were done with their investigations.

"I can see we're also short on surveillance work, too. Nigel, we might have to deploy some cameras. I want to see who is interested in the site other than the police or ATF."

"I can have those rigged tonight. Already started thinking about that. We also have footage inside the lobby area that was saved. All that goes off-site to another server. When the cameras were destroyed, their feed was not."

"Good. I want you combing over those. If you need to hire a couple of helpers, go ahead. And, Kevin, get a couple of your buddies to help with the tracking. Let's find out where Rebecca is and who she's talking to. We have to find Jared and Judie."

"What about Shannon's friend Sandy, Boss? She talks about her all the time. The Cuban makeup artist at the station," reminded Rhea.

"Yes. Kevin, get on that right away."

"Will do."

I surveyed the room. "Where the hell are Ron and Pete? Didn't they get back from their trip to get the princes in New York?"

"Oh, they already have some stories," said Kenny. "I'm pretty sure they are at a couple of strip clubs downtown. The girl they brought with them is a real handful and, I guess, a pretty good lap dancer herself. They asked me, and I agreed probably best to keep them busy, away from their cell phones, and not able to watch the news. Pete didn't want to get the ultimatum from the sultan himself to bring the boys home. They wanted to talk to you."

"Okay, you let Pete and Ron know that they are to not let Khalil and Absalom out of their sight. I'm going to call the sultan tonight, and I'm having surgery in the morning, but as soon as I'm myself again, I want to have a conversation about what we're doing and why, especially now that the project has changed."

I left the last few minutes for questions. Then I told them to go home, get to bed early, and start work at eight, or earlier if they needed to. I wanted them to take notes, so that when I was able, I'd get a status update.

"Before we knew we had some hurdles to go through. Now we know we have an enemy. Believe it or not, that makes it easier. The solution will present itself as soon as we can figure out who that enemy is."

I dismissed the group and called the sultan, who had been in touch with Senator Campbell, been reassured that the princes were safe, and knew I was going to recover.

"I'm rethinking my visit later on," the sultan said.

"Don't do that. You promised."

"Yes, but I didn't expect this."

"Well, let me find out who we are battling first. Then I'll give you the chance to rethink your decision. But don't pull out on me now. Once I get healthy, you know I will protect them with my life."

"You are a man of your word, Marco."

I greeted Dr. Patel one last time before retiring. The night nurse gave me a sedative to help with my sleep. With my pain meds refilled, a new fresh pillow placed on the bed, I began to doze off, dreaming of the warm sand, the beaches, and the sunsets I missed so. Shannon walked beside me, her hair blowing in the gentle moist wind that billowed her skirts and puffed out her blouse. How I wanted endless days of forever with her, just like that. No jets, no bombs, no last-minute rescues. Just building sandcastles on the beach, watching the warm glow of the dying day fall into another bright morning.

My cell was charging by my head, and my screen lit up. I turned and tried to pick up the case, nearly dropping it. The text message was from Shannon's phone number, and at first, my heart was elated.

But then I read the message.

You will never see Shannon again.

Attached to the text message was a picture of her sitting across a table from Jared Newsome.

CHAPTER 13

I SIPPED MY margarita, even though this wasn't a social meeting, as much as Jared would like to think otherwise. It was annoying to me that he kept bringing it up. My filter was getting clogged with all the detritus I'd accumulated—things I learned about people I thought I could trust completely—and now I wasn't sure that filter was even able to function. A clean break from everything, staying away from Marco and the team, staying away from the station and the police, from everybody, seemed the right thing to do until I got my head on straight.

But I did know he was having surgery tomorrow morning. Part of me still wanted to be there at his side. But something was wrong with the whole situation. The fact that he was still paying for Rebecca's bills, which he should have told me, and even suspected Rebecca as being responsible for Em's death chilled my heart. I didn't hate him. I was confused. His empire seemed to be crumbling all around everyone, and I was no longer sure who was the enemy.

That meant I had to get into my journalist research mode—my personal safe space. I needed data. When all else failed, investigating the situation, analyzing the evidence, and looking at the pattern with all the facts at my disposal was the only way I would know for sure. In the meantime, if something didn't add up, that person had to be eliminated from my rolodex for now. Facts don't lie. Emotions do. And there was no doubt in my mind that I still loved Marco and couldn't quite think of him as evil, but somehow, I wasn't sure that he didn't contribute to Emily's accident through his associations with others, namely Rebecca. And how could he be married to someone who would do such a thing? What did that say about him, his judgment, his ability to keep me safe?

As I swirled the strawberry drink around to pick up some of the salt on the rim, I thought about how ironic it was. I had just gotten to the point where I felt I could fully trust him. I'd begun to relax to where I saw that as not only a pleasurable option but a reality. He was the only one who could teach me, set up the framework to keep me safe, and create a position for me at his side.

But when it came right down to it, he didn't trust me with a truth—a deadly and dangerous truth—that changed the whole picture for me. It was my right to know if he suspected someone else was involved in Em's death. It wasn't his secret to keep.

That experience with the man in the pickup was like a burst of reality that my safe bubble was an illusion. Marco even said it was. He was so right. I had to take things under control, learn how to defend myself, and never rely on anyone else one hundred percent to keep me safe. Without my own active involvement, safety was always going to be a fantasy.

Jared had been watching me, and he was now beginning to make me nervous.

"Aren't you even going to look at the information I printed out for you?" he asked.

"I will, when I'm alone. Not here."

"Well, this was your choice, Shannon. Look—" he reached out to touch my hand and I pulled back. "It's not like that."

"Then stop doing it. You freak me out every time you touch me."

"But I'm not the enemy. I'm not the one you should be afraid of."

"Oh, so now you're going to be my security, like Marco thought he could?"

"Shannon, I started to uncover some irregularities with your sister's death. Who else has brought you this kind of information? If you couldn't trust me, why bring me something to do that might endanger me or my position? I care about you, deeply."

"There you go again."

"Now you're being spoiled. Can you afford to select nobody to trust? Really? You ready to carry that load?"

"Clearly I'm not." I sighed, dropped my hands to my lap. "Jared, we're friends. You helping me with this doesn't mean we'll ever be anything but friends. I gotta know you're doing this because you are my friend, not someone who wants a relationship afterwards. When you continually bring up how much you care, you assume I don't see that you want more. But you don't stop telling me, so of course I do. And that bothers me. I'm okay that you want more. Are you okay if there never is any?"

"Maybe you misunderstand me," he whispered.

"Oh, come on. How could I?"

"We are headed into very dangerous territory. You're launching a campaign that might expose you to people who want things kept quiet—not for any nefarious reason, just not to open old wounds or something. I don't know. But I do know this: I agree with what everyone has told you, Marco, Rebecca and probably others. I think you're in danger. If you were the target of the bomb or the fiancé of the person who was, it makes no difference. Your proximity to the source of that danger and the fact that you're pushing away everyone who wants to help you just because you don't trust them is concerning. You have to trust someone."

I smiled. "That's exactly what Marco said."

"He's right. Look, I'm jealous as hell about the guy—"

I drilled him a look that stopped him mid-sentence.

"Okay, I guess I'm trying to convince you like you were a guy or something, because clearly, I'm not getting through. The point is, and this is the only way I can say it, if I'm so jealous of him and I still don't think he's your enemy, maybe you should reconsider that as well. I know I told you earlier not to get him involved, but what if that's a huge miscalculation? You could be setting yourself up for disaster. I don't have to be in love with you to care about whether you wind up in a dump site somewhere with your throat cut."

My first reaction was anger at the suggestion. I couldn't think of anything to say back to him or to refute the logic of his argument.

"There has to be an explanation. You're doing your own research, but you're not involving the one person who is very close to the center of it all. How smart is that, Shannon?"

I was getting tired, and the alcohol was beginning to wear on me with what little I'd eaten today. I needed a good night's sleep to catch up, to be able to think. I knew Marco was probably sending out people to find me, so I might not have a lot of time to do it.

"Okay, I'll take your information, I'll review it tonight. I'll get to bed—get a motel—and crash. I'll call you in the morning. I'll talk to you first before I talk to anyone else."

"Fair enough. I'm still worried. But I won't launch anything until morning. And if you don't call me, I'm going to make a huge noise, so don't do that, okay?"

"I promise."

"One other thing. I think you should leave your car here, in case someone's tracking you, and let me drop you off at a motel that's safe. Please let me do that, Shannon. I will rest better tonight if I know you're checked in safely for the night."

I worried my lack of wheels would make it more difficult to get everything done tomorrow. I had to go to the bank to get a new credit card and some cash, and I had to get some clothes, as I needed to avoid my little house by the beach. But that was where I really wanted to be. But the alternative wasn't much of a problem. I could always get a taxi back here, pick up my car in the morning.

It was a weak moment, I knew. But I was getting tired of fighting all the worry inside my head.

"Okay. I'll do that. I made a reservation without a credit card at the Wyndham in Clearwater. I've been there before."

Jared settled our tab. I picked up the manilla inner-office folder filled with items he'd copied for me, my briefcase with my laptop in it, and the satchel with a change of underwear and some toiletries. I'd left the scrubs at my place, in favor of a fresh pair of jeans and a long-sleeved tee shirt.

The two of us pulled out of the parking lot, which was jammed with people arriving for the evening entertainment and headed north on Gulf Boulevard toward Clearwater.

I LEFT JARED sitting in his car at the lobby entrance. After confirming and checking in, I came back out and waved him off. Then I headed straight for the elevator to the tenth floor, locked the deadbolt, and pulled over the security bar. As I sat in the dark, my emotions welled up, until I began to sob.

It was not exactly the way I expected these few days to go. I was alone, in the dark, and left without re-sources in a sterile room overlooking the breathtakingly beautiful glistening waters of the Gulf of Mexico. Even at night, it was stunning.

How could I have come this low?

I wet a washrag with cool water and wiped my face and neck, examining myself in the mirror. It was a frightful sight. I looked into the face of someone totally out of control.

What have I done?

I tried calling Judie again, and this time, my friend answered. She sounded like she'd just pounded down a good bottle of Scotch, which was her drug of choice.

"Judie, you sound terrible. Are you sick?" I asked.

"Oh God, Shannon, I came down with a migraine and went to bed. I woke up today to a dozen angry calls from Jared. I'm so sorry I worried everyone. And you, you've been through a lot, Shannon. What the hell is going on?"

"You heard about the bomb."

"Yes. Marco's in the hospital. Is he okay? Nobody at the station knows anything. Everyone's running around trying to chase leads, and the whole place is just a mess. Police in and out, some of Marco's guys there—"

"Marco's guys? Who?"

"I think two of his military buddies interviewed me just a half hour ago at the office. They were looking for you. Where have you disappeared to? And why?"

"I'm not sure myself, except I discovered Marco thinks Rebecca might have something to do with Emily's death, as well as the bomb."

"That bitch? No way."

"Well, he thinks so."

"She's a piece of work. But I just think her world's falling apart, and she's lost the war. I mean, Marco belongs to you now. She was up at the station today looking for Jared, like everyone else. She got into a huge argument with a couple of the techs who had her removed. It was bizarre to say the least. I guess she tried to go see Marco but no one would give her entry."

"I was there, I know. So, Judie, I may need your help."

"You got it. But wait, why aren't you at the hospital?"

"I have to check some things out. I'm trying to stay out of sight, looking into the theory that Em's death wasn't a DUI case after all. If I ask you to, would you run some errands for me?"

"Of course. You need anything tonight? I can run out to the beach, no problem."

"I'm not at my house. I took a place up in Clearwater. I needed the space to think and do a little online research." I didn't like lying to my best friend, but I didn't want to reveal too much.

"Okay. Well, I hope you know what you're doing. I mean, Shannon, there's a bomber out there, and it's not safe."

"Tell me about it."

"I don't like the idea you're out there all alone, Shannon. Are you sure you're doing what's smart?"

"I'm just trying to be safe."

I heard a knock on my door, which jolted my senses.

"What was that?" asked Judie.

"Someone's at the door. But only Jared knows I'm here."

"Hotel security, ma'am. We need to speak to you for a second." The muffled message came through.

"Don't open that door, Shannon. Call the police. Better yet, let me call them."

"They say they're hotel security."

"No. Do. Not. Open. That. Door," Judie insisted.

A small explosive charge blew the handle off the door. In my shock, I dropped the phone to the floor. As it swung inside through a small cloud of white smoke, a man dressed in all black entered, charging straight at me. I had nowhere to run, but I tried to protect myself with the TV stand and desk at the foot of my bed. He crashed through, sending the lamp and the monitor to the floor in pieces.

I could still hear Judie screaming on the phone. The man lunged for me, caught me around the waist, and pulled me like a rag doll toward him.

I was keenly aware of the fact that I had no idea what to do to fend this attacker off. He applied pressure with his hand at the side of my neck and the room began to spin, blackness creeping into my vision until there was only a spark left.

My last thoughts were the realization that if I survived this night, I'd never let this happen to me again. I'd learn how to treat my body as a weapon. There was only one person in the world I trusted to teach me how to do that.

And he was lying in a hospital bed trying to find me.

CHAPTER 14

I WAS FRUSTRATED, trying to think and work with my team even though my mind and senses were dulled. Several nurses requested my visitors removed with no luck. Finally, they reached Dr. Patel, who showed up at the door like the Grim Reaper.

"Stop. Stop all this." He surged across the room and stood over the bed, his face about to explode in a flurry of bitter words.

I interrupted his fury. "It's a life-or-death thing. Shannon is in danger." I showed Dr. Patel the picture on my cell. "Even if I wanted to, I won't be able to relax, Doc." My head fell back into the pillow.

"I don't understand how come you're still awake, Marco. You're threatening the surgery and, in a way, threatening your own health and safety. I cannot be responsible for this."

Art stepped forward, introducing himself. "Dr. Patel, this person," he said, pointing to Marco's cell, "texted that picture from Shannon's cell, the same one stolen from the television station yesterday when the bomb went off. That makes a direct connection. We have to find her before he makes good on his promise."

Patel looked at the faces of the five team members who were conferring, taking notes, talking on the phone, or standing at the ready, waiting for instructions.

"Then, if it's that important, we must figure out a quick solution, because this man needs surgery tomorrow morning. If it's postponed, I'm not sure we'll get the same result, and with a full calendar, they may not be able to accommodate him. Just so you understand, you have to wrap this up." He looked at his watch. "I give you twenty minutes only. Then I'm going to make everyone leave, and I'm going to personally confiscate his cell phone."

The room was quiet. Several nurses stood in the doorway awaiting instructions from the doctor. It was a brief standoff.

"That's what we're going to do then," I said. "Get everyone up who can help out. We must find Shannon. I want all of you to re-contact everyone you've been in touch with and check for updates on her sighting. And has anyone reached Jared?"

"I just did," said Rhea. "You want to talk to him, Marco? I got him on speaker."

"Yes." I was feeling fully awake now. I grabbed her cell.

"What the hell's going on there?" Jared shouted.

I ignored him. "Where's Shannon?"

"Well, um…"

"Shut the fuck up and tell me. I have your picture sitting with her at a restaurant. The text underneath said I'd never see her again. So where the fuck is she? If something happens to her, I'm going to personally hold you responsible."

"Oh, geez. That means—"

"Means what?"

Someone from the background shouted out, "I have Judie. She says someone broke into her room."

I screamed across the room, nearly ripping myself out of the bed, "Where?"

"She doesn't know," came the answer.

"Did you hear that? Judie says someone broke into her room." I was ready to launch into another tirade, but Jared blurted out,

"Wyndham Clearwater."

"We're on it. Have the cops meet us there, Rhea," said Forest. Art and Kevin left with him.

"I'll meet them there as well. I didn't anticipate all this," Jared said before he signed off.

I was already giving him a piece of my mind when I discovered Jared was no longer on the line. I felt like I was about to explode. I drew my arm back, the drugs pulling back the veil of my control, intending to throw the phone into the wall.

"Wait!" shouted Rhea. "That's my phone." She yanked it back and handed it to Dax. "Marco, you have to get right in the head. You're not thinking."

Dax looked up at Dr. Patel. "He's not going to hear back in time. You gotta let him stay up until they locate her. Please."

Patel paced the room then turned to Marco. "Give your phone to your crew, Marco. If there is news, I will instruct them to come in and disturb you, let you know."

I shook my head. "No. We have to postpone this surgery. I gotta get out of here. I can't have—"

"Even if you weren't having surgery, the answer is no. You're in a semi-sterile environment here, one I can manage. Even if you could navigate outside, and you can't, you'll move that leg around. You could disturb all the alignments. I'd have to go in and operate again. You run the risk of losing your leg. You were that close," he said, using his fingers to show. "We're building up your blood supply, cutting it close as it is, so no, it's out of the question, what you're thinking. I know what you're going through—"

"Do you?" I barked back.

"Boss, I'll stay right here all night if I have to. The

doc's right. Try to get some rest," pleaded Rhea.

Dax was checking Rhea's phone. "Forest has already contacted hotel security, and the surveillance footage from the lobby area will be available to the team when they get there. They're restricting all movement out of the hotel. Police are five minutes away."

"All right. We've done all we can. I want the two of you out. Marco, your phone…" Dr. Patel held his hand out. I reluctantly gave it up. Dax and Rhea were ushered out, Rhea whispering assurances as she was literally forced from the room.

I was in full-on combat mode but without the weapons and physical ability to get into the fight. Instead of using my brain to strategize and help plan, I was trying to figure out a way to get out of the hospital, which I realized could cost me dearly. I knew this was counterproductive thinking, but with the drugs in my system, I was fighting a losing battle over my consciousness. Patel instructed I be given another sleep aid, which at first only intensified my mental wanderings.

Every single one of my mistakes came flaring to the surface. Yes, I should have told Shannon about the full conversation with Rebecca. I should have demanded someone go follow her. I should have demanded answers from Rebecca that afternoon when they visited her. There were so many things I should have followed up on and didn't.

But the biggest regret, as I fell into a deep sleep, was that I hadn't assigned someone to Shannon's security team immediately. That was a fatal flaw and had the possibility of causing—I didn't want to think about it. I'd been a dumbass, worrying about the project first, when someone was already two steps ahead of me.

And I had no clear idea who or what I was fighting.

CHAPTER 15

I WOKE UP with a skull-splitting headache. I was also sick to my stomach and dizzy. I tried to roll to my side but found I was fully restrained. My panic only escalated when I discovered my mouth had been taped over with duct tape. That meant I could suffocate on my own vomit!

My legs were also bound with duct tape at the ankles, and my hands done the same way behind my back. I tried to push my feet against some surface to right myself since I couldn't use my arms, but when I did, I felt pieces of equipment moving rather than a hard structure to boost from. My ears buzzed with the sound of a heavy-duty diesel motor. I was in the camper shell of a diesel pickup, just like the one I'd seen at the dog park that day!

Another wave of nausea came over me. I inhaled and exhaled deeply, hoping to clear my head while telling myself I was not sick, trying to coax my stomach into submission. I did not have the ability to put my head between my knees, but the deep breathing calmed me, and soon I became distracted by all sorts of ideas and visions.

I took an assessment of my environment. I could hear traffic, like on a freeway. The road was smooth. The equipment my feet had encountered was small enough to slide and it rattled with the rhythm of the truck's bouncing over occasional uneven pavement. I checked all my extremities. Nothing hurt, but the lack of blood circulation to my wrists was painful, making my hands feel warm and swollen. But as I tried, the tape didn't budge.

When I checked my ankle restraints, there was more movement. But after several minutes trying to pry myself free, I couldn't make enough space to get one leg released. So I went back to my hands and, this time, felt something sharp against my fingers. Then I smelled oil or some solvent. From the shape of the sharp metal piece, I identified it as a propeller blade, perhaps a small boat motor. Trying to push it back and forth, I confirmed that it was heavy and began to rub the tape against the edge of the blade until I was able to slice through the tape to free myself.

Next, I removed the tape from my mouth and gasped, inhaling in gulps and becoming sicker, my stomach gurgling in protest as I smelled and almost tasted the thick fumes from the motor in the stifling hot compartment. I didn't have much in my stomach, so when I involuntarily vomited, all I gave up was a sickening, bitter bile.

I was able to sit up at last, leaning over to unbind my ankles, rubbing them to increase circulation.

I became aware that lights flashed occasionally through tiny windows in the side of the camper shell, figuring out they were streetlamps as we drove by. As the light illuminated the contents of the camper, I recognized pieces of camera equipment that looked vaguely familiar. Several heavy black electrical cords were in the corner, wrapped in coils and strapped with Velcro ties. On the side of the body of the camera was a decal. Upside down, I read the letters: TMBC.

I instantly recognized the camera and the operator from my last broadcast. The assistant producer had made some creepy point about having me smile and look pretty for the viewers. Was this the person who had been stalking me? And could he be the bomber? Was he hired by someone else?

Scanning the area, I looked for a weapon. The cords were too thick to use for anything. The camera was too bulky, and I doubted I could even lift it. But beneath my feet I noticed two metal rods, part of a boom assembly to hold up a microphone from a ceiling location. They had been unscrewed and laying side by side, and when I picked one up, it felt light enough to wield and heavy enough to do damage.

The truck was pulling off the freeway, but instead of stopping, it exited onto a paved surface with pot-holes, and the driver slowed down.

Who was he? I had worked at the station for some time but never saw his face. Perhaps he was new, but in the environment I was in, the surrounding area was mostly dark when we filmed, all the lights being directed at the podium. I never had occasion to speak with the crew except Sandy, my makeup artist. In fact, I couldn't recall any of their faces and probably wouldn't recognize them in public.

When the truck tires thumped off pavement and onto a gravel road, my pulse spiked. Now, if I managed escape, I'd be in a more remote area, probably some area the driver was familiar with. On a freeway or main road with streetlamps, I had more of a chance of stopping a passer-by or witness. Listening for other signs of life, I heard no other vehicles running.

Off in the distance, I heard a siren, which quickly passed by without slowing down or stopping, but that gave me a directional signal back to a traveled main road of some kind. If I could somehow get away, that's where I would head to.

Thunder clapped suddenly, and I almost screamed. It was followed by the sounds of heavy droplets falling on the top of the shell. The smell of the rain hitting hot, humid soil was the only thing familiar about my surroundings. But then, that's what all of Florida felt like in the middle of rainy season.

I felt the speed of the truck begin to slow, so I picked up the metal pole and fiddled with the back window, latched from the outside. If I launched the pole and broke the glass, the driver would know I'd gotten myself untied and would be forewarned. And the glass would be tricky to maneuver through without getting seriously cut. So I waited.

I wondered if Marco's team was even aware that I'd been taken, since they didn't know I went to the hotel in the first place. I remembered dropping the burner phone during my conversation with Judie, but the only person who knew where I'd gone was Jared.

No, I thought, I was on my own. It was by my own design. Again, another bad decision made of haste. My lack of trust in Marco had caused this whole problem, just like his lack of trust in me exacerbated things when he didn't divulge information he was withholding from me about Em's death.

Playing back all the elements of today, I remembered Rebecca trying to restrain me at the hospital, desperate, clutching, and saying over and over, "You're in danger."

Did Rebecca hire this person, who now was going

rogue? And was it even possible the two of them could be involved in Emily's death? And what did that say about Marco, being married to a murderess for fifteen years? Wouldn't he know she had a secret blood sport?

The truck brakes squealed, and then the truck's forward momentum stopped. It was time to get ready. I lifted the pole gingerly, readying myself to strike given the opportunity. I heard footsteps crunching on the gravel surface, heard the latch on the shell being turned, and finally felt the cool, moist air as the lid to my dungeon was raised.

One quick jab to the man's upper sternum sent him reeling backward, but he scrambled to right himself, howling in pain. I slipped my legs through the opening and dropped to the ground. My feet were covered in mud all the way to my ankles.

Then I ran.

By the light of the moon, I sifted through dense foliage, stepping into little tidepools filled with who knew what. I didn't even want to think about predators in the area: coyotes, crocs, snakes, and other animals that could be deadly. But I held onto my pole and used it to poke areas I was afraid to step in.

The sound of rustling leaves and branches told me he was following right after me. I knew I would not be able to outrun him, that this area was probably some familiar place for him, putting me at a disadvantage. If

I were captured again, I likely wouldn't survive the second ordeal, so I crept behind bushes and through ponds to avoid capture. I hoped to at least get closer to the roadway to seek help. If I found somewhere, I could hunker down until morning, where light would be my friend.

When I no longer heard the brush moving in the distance, I stopped to take stock of where I might be. That's when I recognized the sound of rushing water but not like from a river or stream. It was coming from a spillway of some sort at my feet, and I sensed a steep gorge below. Using the pole for balance, I slid down the bank beside the metal culvert, not sure how far it would drop, until I found an area below it that was dry and formed a sort of cave.

Wind started blowing rain into the opening. I moved as far back as I could, still clutching the pole in my now muddy hands, hugging my legs together to make a small ball, and leaned back as far against the back of the opening as possible. I was rewarded with the wonderful feeling of warmth and the smell of moist loamy soil falling all around me and giving me partial shelter from the cold air. Though the rain was heavy, the surface of the terrain remained warm from the hot sun of that afternoon. I leaned into the wall of mother nature's womb and felt safe for the first time in hours.

CHAPTER 16

SUNLIGHT POURED THROUGH the hospital window, covering my upper forehead and scalp. I blinked then tried to cover my eyes, but I realized my right hand was already hooked up to an I.V. I was confused and startled for a few seconds until I remembered this was my surgery day. I turned my head away, searching for anyone else in the room, and found it empty. After a brief search, I pushed the buzzer.

Several minutes later, one of the floor nurses came in with Rhea right behind her. Both were smiling. I was starved for some good news.

"They found her, Marco. Early this morning, Kevin and Forest located her hiding in a water culvert."

"Is she all right? Did they hurt her?"

"She's fine. Scared and a little scraped up. She apparently ran through a tule lake and got some enormous bug bites, but nothing that won't heal quickly. Kevin says she actually looked pretty good for what she's been through."

"Thank God." I took in a deep breath and blew it out, as if that was the end to a very long and painful chapter. "I suppose she's still angry at me?"

"Not on your life, Boss. She's grateful they found her. And she knew you'd send out the dogs after her. We caught the guy too. Art and his buddies located his truck, which had gotten stuck in the mud. We had one hell of a rainstorm last night. He was trying to make his way back to the highway on foot when the Coast Guard chopper located him, and Art and the guys picked him up."

"Who the hell was he?"

"He's the lead cameraman at TMBC for the evening news. Turns out, he has some history. I'll let the boys tell you about it."

"But what about Rebecca?"

"She tried several times to come back here and talk to you. I managed to convince her to tell me what was so important. She knew this guy was a whacko, had run into him on the street when he told her he was working on some breaking news regarding your project. He told her he was a reporter there. She spilled the beans on all kinds of stuff about you and Shannon, what she knew anyway, and that's how he figured out how to get to her. Technically, Rebecca is an accessory, but I think she didn't realize she was being used until she ran into him at the station, looking for Jared."

"I'm not holding my breath. I don't think her claws retract. She's still committed to ruining me for some reason."

"Woman spurned."

"Except she did the turning away. I don't buy that for a minute."

"Well, just forget about it. You've got to get ready for your big day and then, after that, a reunion with Shannon. So I just wanted to let you know. Decided since it was good news, I'd let you sleep. Doctor's orders."

"Thanks. Where's Dax?"

"She went over to be with Shannon. I mean, the cops must take pictures and process everything. She's in for an ordeal before she can get cleaned up and get some rest. I guess Shannon's friend Judie is meeting them at the station to help as well. She's got good support. She'll be fine. You worry about you."

I looked at the nurse who was injecting something through my I.V. "This is to help with the surgery, so just relax. Dr. Patel will be in shortly. We'll get you down to surgery right after. How do you feel?"

"Hungry."

"Any pain?"

I looked between my legs. Rhea scrunched up her nose and upper lip. "Ouch," she said.

"Well, I'm sorry. Can't do anything about that unless you want me to look. I can pull the curtain," the nurse said with a smirk.

"No, thank you. I'll have the doc do it." My irritation was rising. I wanted my life back.

"How are the princes?" I asked Rhea just before Dr. Patel entered.

"Sleeping off a bender. You owe Pete and Ron a nice, quiet vacation after this. With the girl, I guess it was quite a scene."

"But no trouble, right?"

"Reckless but no trouble. Honestly, for being bright guys, they sure don't seem to act like it. We're to call over there when you're out of surgery. I think they've been instructed to pay their respects."

"Just what I need."

"Except you're gonna have Shannon back, Boss. That makes a difference, doesn't it?"

"If she'll have me."

Dr. Patel, who had been writing in my chart, moved closer to the bed. "Okay, Marco. We're ready. I understand the team had success last night. So, all's well with your future?"

"I hope so."

"Looks like you're going to owe some pretty big thank yous. I'm glad it worked out. So now we must focus on the next big hurdle. There is always the chance that the knee repair will result later in a total knee replacement, but we'll see how well I can get you fixed up. And there is always the possibility this new surgery will exacerbate the femur stabilization. So let's keep our fingers crossed. You think about all the good things in your life you have to look forward to, except perhaps running marathons, and ask your little healing angel to give you a hand."

"Angel?"

"The one who held your femoral artery together until I could get in there and repair it."

"Oh, that one. Will do." I didn't have a clue what he was talking about. I began to feel sleepy and noticed, late, the nurse had added something else to my drip.

"I'm going to get prepared, and I'll meet you down-stairs. Wave to all your fans along the way. It will take your mind off the procedure."

I was getting confused. Rhea looked like she had two heads, and then my eyes got very sleepy. A warm feeling overcame my body as the pain in my leg and knee drifted off into space. Just as I was told, as they wheeled me through the doorway and down the hall to the elevator, I waved to all the imaginary fans in the wings.

"You got this, Boss. We'll all be here when you come back!" Rhea's voice got smaller and smaller until I couldn't hear anything but the squeaking of the wheels on the gurney.

The two male orderlies working the head and foot of the gurney were whispering.

"You got plans for lunch?" one asked the other.

"The burger basket was all I planned. You can come," the other one answered.

I barked, "That is so unfair," just before I fell asleep.

MY FIRST SENSE that I was still alive was I heard laughing. Of course, they'd be laughing. I only hired people with a good sense of humor, and the boss was always the brunt of all the jokes. I tried to count the laughs, since there were no words being spoken and people were trying desperately *not* to laugh.

I must have moved, because someone shushed everyone to silence. I expected them to say something like, "Let the king speak," but of course, that was ridiculous.

At last, the mystery was killing me, so I opened my eyes and let the smiles in the room come fall all around me. God, it was great to be alive, I thought. That was something to smile for.

Just as promised, Khalil and Absalom were right there, without their normal silk pajama attire. No jewelry either. Each of them wore a pair of Hawaiian print golfing shorts in solid blue and green and bright matching Aloha shirts with pineapples, flamingos, and old 1950's vintage convertible cars with surfboards coming out of the back seat. They looked like they were having a good time. Each sported a big grin.

"Boss!" said Khalil, who reached over and grabbed my hand in a grip, not a shake. Absalom was a bit shyer to adopt the custom, but his warm, eager expression told me everything.

"Father sends his respects for a smooth and easy recovery, Marco. He wishes that you reschedule his boot camp," Absalom stated in a formal, clipped Indian dialect.

I began to feel hot pain coming from my upper leg and twisted a bit to try to elevate my knee, but my entire leg had been immobilized. I closed my eyes. "Just a minute. I'm having a hard time getting the right position."

Dr. Patel introduced himself, and the two boys dialogued with him in Hindi. Then he gave his attention to me. "It's normal to start to feel pain right now. I've ordered you something for it, which should be here soon."

"I forgot that part, Doc," I whispered.

"Maybe I have something better for the pain," Patel said softly.

Shannon appeared at my bedside. Her pink cheeks and soft red lips looked so fresh and inviting. Her timid smile made even my toes, which hadn't recovered from the anesthetic yet, tingle.

"Hey there, sweetheart," I said, my eyes filling up with water. "God, I owe you a lifetime of apologies. I misjudged everything. I almost lost you."

"But you didn't. I'm here, and I have much to apologize for as well. But I like the lifetime of saying whatever it is you want to say to me. I promise I'll listen. I'll hang on every word, as long as you get back to your perfect, ornery self and start chasing me around with your cane."

"A cane is it, Doctor? You didn't tell me about that," I said as Shannon bent down and kissed me gently on the lips. "Ah, paradise. I've been to paradise."

I watched Shannon blush and waited for the doctor's response.

"We'll see. I wouldn't bet against you, Marco. But let's be patient. Your body has been through a lot of stress. No ordinary person would be expected to get up and start dancing. But somehow, for you, it will be different. I'm sure you'll be breaking records, my man."

I held Shannon's hand while Rhea and Dax greeted me next. Then Forest and Kevin entered with Art right behind.

"I understand you guys found this little worm in a storm drain?"

"Not quite, Marco. She was hiding in a cave underneath it. Very smart little lady," said Art.

Shannon squeezed my hand. "Lucky for me, it happened in Florida, where the ground is warm, even in the rain. It kept me toasty until morning. I fell asleep. Of course," she showed me the several dozen bites on her forearms and neck, "I think I slept with some other creatures, too, who extracted their bounty on me."

"So who was this guy? Rhea told me he was a cameraman at TMBC?"

Art nodded. "I have a former profiler friend who now does something safer, and she told me it sounded like a fan gone crazy. That didn't make sense, because at the time, we were thinking Rebecca, and she wasn't a fan."

"That's for sure," Kevin mumbled.

"A fan of who, me or Shannon?" I wanted to know.

"A fan of Shannon's. And it turns out, my friend was right, although it didn't help us solve the case. We got him from the surveillance tapes at the hotel, and, well, let's just say he chose the wrong place to show up. Gulf Boulevard has more security cameras than New York," he said.

"Yup, and we were able to track him all the way north until he came to the entrance to Honeymoon Island State Park. Parts of it are rural. The park was closed, but he must have known the terrain, because we think he was headed to an abandoned Ranger Station there. It's dotted with little trails and picnic pavilions all over the place, amongst the virgin slash pine stands, which is what got her all cut up. If she'd have kept running, she'd have made it to the beach," added Kevin.

"We owe the Coast Guard a thank you for finding his pickup, or it would have taken us a day or two to comb through the area on foot," Art continued. "We thought we'd find her or him with the night vision the chopper has, but no luck with that. She was safe and sound in that cave."

"So what was his story?"

"He's from California and did work in Santa Rosa. Fancied himself a director of sorts, but his specialty was gory car wrecks. Worked for the newspaper up there, mostly freelance work. When Emily's accident occurred, he covered the funeral, everything. He hounded the drunk driver for years, even getting arrested for confronting him after he got out. The driver only served about five years."

I squeezed Shannon's hand. She was looking down at the bed.

Art continued, "And we think he became obsessed with Shannon. Like he thought he was her protector. He followed her to Florida, knew about her modeling and acting career, and even tried to get hired on as an extra. He'd been planning this for a long, long time,

Marco. He was one mixed-up dude."

"So how did he get the position at TMBC?" I asked.

"He had a fairly decent resume, lots of crime footage, courtroom drama. He tried his hand working with starlets, mostly encouraging them to do skin flicks, but he was not really making money, so when Shannon got the part-time position at the station, he went in and got hired. I guess he had talent and lots of experience. But he was more of a tabloid guy. Probably missed his calling."

"We think that's where his obsession blossomed," added Kevin. "He sort of had her all to himself right under everybody's noses."

"And I never noticed him."

Art nodded her way. "He sure knew a lot about you. We found all kinds of photos and notes. He'd probably been stalking you for some time. Got some racy bedroom scenes, Marco. I'm sure they'll come up at trial."

I tried to smile but felt my blood pressure start to shoot up as the pain level rose to an alarming level. "Doc, I need those meds now."

I was given something in my drip line, which didn't take more than a few seconds to calm me down, and all was right with the world again.

Art added, "We're still looking for the bomber. So far, this guy is not saying a word. We have to be prepared it could be two separate people."

"So the investigation continues, then."

"We'll get him, Boss," added Rhea. "So far, the police don't think Rebecca had anything to do with it either. But they're combing through lots of evidence. I think your stalker fellow is an opportunity player. One down, one to go."

I had so much to feel grateful for, I didn't want this new worry to spoil my joy. But the team wouldn't let me down, and they wouldn't stop, either, until it was solved. I had to trust them, for now. My job was to keep Shannon safe.

Nigel stepped forward. "I got some beautiful surveillance photos with the drone. Of course, I was following the wrong girl for half a day. You didn't tell me Rebecca was now a red head."

"Oops."

"Well, sir, we'll be more than ready next time. My drone worked like a charm. I've got some features I can't wait to show you. I'm hoping to be able to use it when we lift off for Africa."

I was nodding my head, noticing the enthusiasm from the brothers. "Our father says perhaps the trip has been moved up to spring?"

"I don't know. We have work to do here, obviously. I have a bit of a bone to pick with you two about your behavior."

The princes wiped the smiles off their faces.

"Just because we are living in the United States right now doesn't mean you forget your noble birthright. Remember, you are an example of your father's kingdom, and as such, you can wear bright clothes and go out dancing and drinking if he allows it, but you must always think of your mothers. Consider that they are sitting to the side watching you."

The news wasn't greeted warmly, so I decided to do one more rub.

"If that doesn't work, we could always bring them over and do it real-time. Understood?"

"Yes, sir," they both said in unison.

"Where is—" I spotted Pete and Ron, who had become their babysitters for two days, leaning against the hospital room wall. They quietly shuffled over to the bed. Pete pointed a finger at me.

"You owe us big time."

"So I've been told."

"I haven't had so much alcohol since I was a freshman in high school," said Ron. "I'm off the clock for at least seventy-two hours, man."

"Duly noted. And where's the young lady?"

The tiny dancer was beautiful, with dark skin, long black hair, and bright blue eyes. She was barely five feet tall. She took my hand and bowed. Her gold bangles and anklets tinkled delicately. "Sir."

I looked at Ron and Pete. "You sure about her?"

"What? Her age? She's twenty-five," said Ron. "She has a passport now, but it was verified with her mother."

"Somebody's looking for her. That's what I meant. No more of this," I barked. "We don't—"

"I am of the age of consent. I was already a widow at sixteen years of age, sir," she said in perfect English.

Ron and Pete shrugged. Ron added, "They're here, they're legal now, permissions secured where necessary, and everyone's happy. They're ready to work, Marco. Pete and I talked about the jobs they'll be doing, helped them get things for their condo, the one their father bought. We showed them the beaches, some of the places we ate and drank, what was left of the office, and bought them both a computer and a new cell phone. Their dad paid the bills. They're set. I think they're ready."

"And so are we," added Pete.

The room laughed.

I smiled back at the young girl, Selima. "Welcome to Florida. We hope you like our paradise."

"Thank you, sir." She gave a slight nod and retreated to the back of the crowd with her two companions.

I thanked everyone. Shannon had tried several times to give me the use of my hands by letting go, but I grabbed her back each time. This time I winked at her and threw her an imaginary kiss, mouthing *I love you.*

"Okay, I'm afraid showtime is over, ladies and gentlemen. Marco needs rest, and he can't do that with an audience." Dr. Patel turned to me. "I've been told that Shannon now has your cell phone."

"That's fine by me."

"If you would like to stay, my dear, you can sit over there while we do a little dressing change and check out his vitals."

The crowd disbursed into the hallway. I still had so many questions to ask, but I lay back, staring at Shannon's shining face before me. I was going to set things in motion to make sure, if anything like this happened again, no matter how unexpected it may be, that there was a protocol to follow that neither of us deviated from. This time, we'd been lucky, and due to the skill of my team and her quick thinking, the outcome was a happy one.

But next time, we'd be prepared. I had a lot of making up to do, and I couldn't wait to get started.

CHAPTER 17

Four Months Later

I ARRANGED THE table with fresh frangipani blossoms floating in shallow bowls and lit candles creating a cascade of warm light nearly as bright as the sunset at the horizon, which tonight was flaming a deep rose and purple.

The first floor of the house was built, raised on concrete stilts to withstand hurricane force tides and winds. The structure would be concrete block but covered in a warm light green stucco we'd picked out. Framed in white painted pine, with plantation-type shutters, and Hawaiian gingerbread trim along the upstairs decking, it was indeed going to be the house of my dreams. But right now, it was just a floor on stilts, with partial walls on one side overlooking the perfect sunset and beach at Indian Rocks.

I still loved coming home to my little bungalow and never planned to do a thing with it, except clean it up after storms and occasionally rent it out. I planned to keep it as a reminder of where I started, the simple life I adopted when I first came to Florida after the death of Emily.

At the top of the walls, iron bars extended another fifteen feet up into the air, looking like antenna on a spaceship. They were wrapped and tied off to hold them in place until the concrete blocks were set around them. The upstairs platform was to be the huge master bedroom suite with views nearly one hundred and eighty degrees wide and a gingerbread deck as wide as the entire house to sit by candlelight and watch whatever the gulf gave them.

But tonight, we were in the living room, getting ready for the gourmet meal prepared by a private chef downstairs in the dunes. Marco was talking to the gentleman about all the places in the world he'd traveled and what brought him to Florida, always interested in people and their pasts. Beyond the two men were a team of guards, well-hidden in the dunes and along the beach here and there. It was a necessity that had to be, our admission price to living the lifestyle we wanted here.

He looked up at me and raised his wine glass. His tanned face and neck contrasted with the white muslin shirt he wore, his dark and silvery hair blowing in the breeze. If there ever was a picture of a Greek god in the flesh, Marco was him. His body had healed. He stood straight, his massive shoulders wide and firm with just a slight limp and only occasionally using his cane. I had never seen him happier, loving the project we were both working on and making the most of our new life together.

He'd hired several specialists to help me with my training, both weapons as well as self-defense and defensive driving courses. We'd sparred against each other one-on-one when he got strong enough and after I'd been working with the trainers. On occasion, I'd been able to land a good blow to my handsome hero, which delighted me to no end. I began to love the physical conditioning and getting my body into shape. I'd even teased him about rescuing him some day.

My first question, when the subject of Rebecca came up and the police cleared her, was why he paid for her car maintenance.

"I never knew I was. It was set up on an automatic billing. We all missed it. She wasn't going to tell, of course. But I've stopped that and put your little car on the account instead."

Marco and David, our chef, looked like long-lost friends. Their conversation was animated. They kidded with each other and probably told war stories of their different lives. It was fun to watch Marco throw his head back and laugh. He was no longer the troubled, tense former anything—whether it be a SEAL or billionaire. He was just the Marco I loved, working on things he loved in a place he loved.

The chef insisted he bring the platter of grilled vegetables and seafood up the steps himself. Marco was still careful about walking up and down stairs without his cane, but tonight, he used it for balance, since these stairs did not yet have handrails.

David laid the platter down amongst the flowers and candles, explained the variety of fish and shellfish he'd grilled, pointed out the vegetables, and motioned to several dipping sauces he had prepared, some with yogurt and others with spicy oiled mixtures, tamponades, and sauces. Beneath the table, he'd brought some of his signature whole wheat French bread in a large, unsliced loaf. He held it up over the dinner feast and broke it in two, handing one to Marco and the other to me.

"You have butter here as well. But it's excellent for soaking up all these lovely juices. Have fun!"

With that, he bowed, left down the stairs, and drove away slowly.

"Wow!" I squealed. "I have never seen anything so beautiful. Even crab, small pieces of corn on the cob, and sausage."

"He said the sausage is very hot," Marco reminded me.

"I think I'll try some crab and butter, with some bread." I broke a piece off, used a pair of tongs to place the crab meat on the butter-soaked bread, and tasted the orgasmic flavor of the grilled meat enhanced by the ocean salt air and the gentle wind flowing onshore.

Marco watched me, his chin in the palm of his hand, not interested in doing anything but observing me enjoy my food.

I stopped. "What? Is something wrong?"

"Absolutely nothing's wrong. What could possibly be wrong?"

"Don't you want to just dive in?" I asked him.

"No. I want to watch you do it first. I will, trust me. I will."

He took my hand across the table and kissed my palm. Tracing the lifelines coursing back and forth there, he said, "Tell me about the angel. Dr. Patel said there was an angel who helped him fix me. Did you see anything like that?"

He looked up and directly into my eyes. His gaze could not be denied. He wanted an answer.

I stopped chewing, swallowing hard. Staring back, I took a deep breath and whispered, "It was Em, Marco. I could feel her when I asked that she help you. I told her it was too soon for you to join her again. I asked her to send you back. And she did."

Marco stopped tracing my lines but, other than

that, didn't react. "Not exactly. I came back of my own choice. I didn't sense her at all, but I don't doubt that you did. And I think she knew I wanted to stay, to stay with you."

I watched his face illuminated by the orange and red sky, soaking it all in. My eyes filled with grateful tears. I could hardly express what I was feeling.

"You came back for me?" I felt ridiculous for asking but wanted to hear it one more time.

"You are the light of my life. We were made to be together, Shannon. I came back because you are the only one I have ever truly loved. It will always be that way."

I was speechless. So he added, "It's where I belong, where I've always belonged."

I didn't want to break the magic of the moment, but I needed to tell him what was in my heart. "I knew this, what we have now, would be my destiny right from that day you gave me the flower from her grave. I felt it, not like a twelve-year-old, but as the full-grown woman I am today. I saw this day, felt it in my heart, deep inside my bones. I never forgot that feeling growing up, even as I was grieving Emily's passing. I held onto it in that special place reserved for only you. It sustained me, Marco. And it drew me back to you. I had to see if it was real. And it was."

He turned to face the gulf, tears streaming down

his cheeks.

I sat back, both hands now folded in my lap, unsure how to proceed. He was searching the horizon, and then finally, he spoke. "I think what makes life so special is that it doesn't last forever. It's rare. And so beautiful. And love is worth all the risk. It's worth protecting. I'm going to make an artform out of it, Shannon."

We picked at our food then placed the tray back in the zipper case provided by the chef. Otherwise, we'd be sharing it with the sea birds later. Hot lemon-scented towels had been provided, which I felt I needed all over, but it did the job on my hands, forearms, and face.

Marco came around the table and took my hand, walking us both down the stairs of our new dream home, to the dunes and the surf beyond. There was just enough light to make out the outlines of the clouds and still see some stars beginning to pop out of the deep turquoise of the sky.

The surf was warm on our bare feet. No one else was on the beach, yet we knew there were protectors in the dunes. Two tall white egrets and a battered old sea gull studied the waves, perhaps waiting for someone to come for a visit from the ocean.

His tender embrace and kiss lingered a lifetime. My knees were weak. Water splashed up to my knees, and I didn't care. My arms wrapped around his body. "I'm never letting you go," I whispered.

"You couldn't push me away. Not possible."

We'd worked hard these past four months. Diligent with his exercises, his bones had healed, and the terrible gashes that were stitched up completely covered over. All the scarring remained, but he could walk straight. His hip and knee no longer bothered him, and he continued with his PT work to such an extent he was cleared to do some weighted squats and possibly some running eventually. But slowly, day by day, he was recovering even better than before.

The Trident Towers was filling up fast with reservations. Some vet groups came to help with the construction, sometimes for a day or two, sometimes for a week. Our development group had helped train other construction companies and developers to copy our plan and facilitate having towers built in their communities. It was the best kind of giving back I could think of. Khalil and Absalom became used to giving interviews, even drumming up support for the upcoming project in Africa, which they were proud to be made construction managers of.

I thought about all these things as we ascended the stairs again and sat on the top step.

"Who knew Khalil and Absalom would turn out to be great team members? What a rocky start they had,"

I whispered. "I think of all the arguments they had with our team to begin with."

"They had to learn that respect is something you earn, not what you're born into. That was a hard lesson for them. I could have easily sent them back for attempting to fire trusted members of our group. And I let them know, if they made me choose between them and my team, I'd chose my team any day. They had to hear and confront that."

"You think they really learned it?" I asked.

"We taught that too. Fake it until you make it. That lesson was easier for them." Marco chuckled. "Easier than staying out of strip clubs and being too forward with the ladies, at least."

"They love to surf."

"I think that kept them here when nothing else could. Yup, they manned up real good. I'm proud of them."

The wedding had been planned for January, only two months away. All the invitations were mailed out, and all the details of the wedding were worked out by the sultan's wives. I knew there would be some surprises and new adventures waiting for us when we arrived at the Pink Palace.

"I can't wait for the wedding. Are you nervous?" I asked him.

"It's a big step, isn't it? But no, this is how to do it

right. Make a big festival out of it. Celebrate with all those you love. I think I learned that from the sultan himself."

As a gesture of good will, I had even consulted with Rebecca on some of the lobby decorations, but Rebecca was not given a credit card nor a checkbook or authorization to spend. I enjoyed working with her. Knowing Marco like I did, I knew it would be impossible for Rebecca not to still be in love with him, and I made my peace with it. Rebecca's ticket of admission was that she behaved, never got in the way, and never exerted her will over any member of the team. And Marco insisted that she not be paid for any of her work, either. The truce had held.

"I'm ready to turn in. How about you?"

I nodded.

They left the candles to blow out on their own and walked to the back of the platform where a large pillow bed had been placed this afternoon. Inside the bed was a layer of lavender infused in the foam.

I searched for evidence of their guards as Marco began removing my dress over the top of my head.

"I told them not to look."

"But I'm"—and as he pulled the dress away, I finished—"naked!"

He wrapped his arms around me and helped me into the soft sheets and lavender scent. "Only to my eyes. You are soft and naked," he said as he stroked me, "and a pleasure to touch, to kiss, and to love." His fingers laced through my hair as he kissed my neck and down between my breasts.

It was a warm night. I watched the stars above him as he slowly worked his magic, brought me bliss, and set us both on fire.

His hands, mouth, and tongue showed me the need I filled for him. He demanded all of me. I needed him deep, setting me ablaze and then letting me float through the clouds with my fingers and legs entangled in his, holding on to forever with all the intensity of a forever dream.

We were and always would be made for each other.

CHAPTER 18

THE SULTAN OF Bonin had done everything he could do to avoid coming for the promised visit to Florida. I wasn't going to let him forget that promise, and knew that once made, it was a life-or-death thing for the sultan.

He'd been instructed not to bring more than one or two wives, but as Shannon and I waited for them to deplane, I could see the sultan had violated the first rule in the style to which he was accustomed. He brought six wives, each with their own servants plus servants for the servants to carry all the clothing and equipment they required.

The sultan stood in the doorway of the private jet entrance and held his hands out to the side with a frown. He was asking for forgiveness already. I thought to myself, I should have known better, but this meant another eight-bedroom house would have to be procured just to lodge everyone.

I approached him and hesitated to give him a hug in public. But the sultan initiated it, grabbing me by the upper arms and examining me from head to toe.

"You are strong and well, Marco. I can't believe it. You are bigger and stronger than before."

"Good to see you, sir. I can see you followed my instructions," I replied, noticing the bevy of women congregated in the doorway, waiting for permission to enter the lobby area.

"You know women, Marco. I tried to choose the oldest wives first and the younger ones objected. I tried to figure a lottery system where it was random, and they refused. Luckily, several didn't want to come and told me they would never in their lives wear a bathing suit and expose themselves to strangers. But that didn't solve the whole problem."

I knew he didn't try very hard to cull the entourage.

"I expected this to happen. I just didn't think there would be so many. We'll make it work somehow."

"They don't all need separate bedrooms, you know. They are used to sleeping all together. The servants too."

"I understand. Do you want to ask them to enter? It's hot in the breezeway."

I presented Shannon, who was greeted by the sultan warmly, as well as the wives.

As we walked through the small concourse, private

jet passengers stared as the crowd passed by as if they were watching the U.S. President and his staff arriving.

My earpiece squawked. "You think six more Suburbans will do?" Kevin asked.

"Hopefully. How fast can you get them?" I asked.

"We had them on standby, so they're here."

"Thanks. That earns you a bonus, Kevin."

The sultan looked puzzled.

"I have an earpiece so I can talk to my team. This is a large group. I wanted to be sure we had enough transportation."

"They can wait. That is no problem."

"I've arranged it. It's all done."

"Excellent."

Shannon and I rode in the car with the sultan, who elected not to have part of his group with him. I knew it was because he needed to discuss something that he didn't want known. I braced for another surprise.

"My health is not very good right now. I had a physician who specializes in cancer research come in and take a battery of tests and evaluate me. There is some alternative treatment available, but he fears I'm too far past that point."

"You have lung cancer?"

"Confirmed."

"Then have surgery."

"I don't want surgery. I don't like the recovery time."

"But if you don't, they'll just watch you fade away. It could be a long process and more painful than the surgery. I wish you'd reconsider."

"I think I've made my decision to do nothing. I want to see my sons go to Africa and come back successful businessmen before I go. Perhaps see them marry too?"

"But why cut your life short?" I was stunned at his decision.

The sultan watched the Florida landscape through the window as they zoomed past beaches, palm trees, and stopped for beachgoers in wagons with little children in tow.

"So this is Florida. Much different than I thought. I was expecting Miami Vice. Corvettes and bright pink and turquoise buildings and lots of neon lights."

"No, that's a bit south, and we can visit there, but not with a group this size and not with you wearing your fine clothes," I pointed to his gold pajamas studded on the chest with jewels which he wore like medals.

"The world is changing, Marco. There are fewer and fewer kingdoms like Bonin every year. Some of them perish because of bad decisions in business or changes in global politics, shipping rules, and governments. Friends die, policies change. And all the while, there are bad women out there who sometimes cause kingdoms to fall as well."

He looked up at me as if judging my reaction. "But you're rock solid." And then he gave a belly laugh. "But we're only as good as our healthy family. Family is everything. But they are all leaving. They can see the writing on the wall. The ones who want to stay don't work. I find myself supporting more and more of them every year. It is not a sustainable situation."

"I'm sorry to hear that."

"Don't be. It's what I choose. I want to go out on top! I don't need to watch it all fall into the ocean. I don't want to know who will inherit my throne. I will be the last Sultan of Bonin. And then, I'd like my family to do something good with it, in memory of me."

I was touched with his kindness and the fact that I'd been entrusted with an important secret I had to keep.

"Shannon and I will not say a word to anyone. But thank you for honoring your promise. Considering the circumstance, you didn't have to do it. You could have told me."

"Nonsense! I'm not dead yet." He stared at a road worker holding an orange sign that read STOP. "Does he do that all day. Doesn't he get hot?"

"They have rest breaks, and they drink a lot of water."

"Stop, stop please," he shouted to the driver, who had been given the go-ahead to proceed.

"Pardon?" asked the driver.

Before I could intervene, the sultan asked, "Do we have any bottled water with us?"

"Yes, there are several in the chest at your feet."

"Excellent. You wait right here."

The sultan cracked the lid, picked up four bottles of water, opened the door to the Suburban, nearly tripping on his gold pajamas, ran to the man with the orange sign, and presented them to him. The road worker looked at the sultan as if he was a green man from Mars. Shannon and I couldn't tell what he was telling the worker, but he waved and came back to the car. A long line of cars behind him started honking.

"Sir, you must be strapped in before I can go," said the driver.

"Marco, help me with this."

I attached the belt, and the entourage was allowed to proceed.

WE PULLED UP to a massive pink stucco home on a triple lot facing the beach and gulf beyond. One by one, the passengers were dropped off. I helped the sultan up the steps, which he had difficulty with. At the top, he wheezed and took a moment to catch his breath.

"I'm not sure this house will work for me," he said.

I kicked myself for forgetting about the elevator on the backside and informed him of it. "It goes between all three floors. There's a beautiful pool out this way too. And..."

The two front doors swung open, and Khalil and Absalom were standing in their bare feet inside on the marble tile floor. They both wore their favorite Jams shorts and Florida-themed tee shirts. Absalom's orange shirt had a big green alligator on it with the word "SNAP" on the front.

"My boys!"

Both came to him and took turns giving him a hug.

"Father, we have shorts for you too."

"Oh, this doesn't have to happen. Let me get my breath and look at this place first. We can talk about beach attire later."

"But you must. It's tradition. You're in Florida now."

"Not in front of the women," he whispered.

Everyone could hear squealing as the ladies were let out of their cars, chattering with each other and with their servants. The drivers stood at attention, stoically attending to their needs. Luggage was pulled out of a large white van filled to the top with various bags belonging to the different wives and their party.

The sultan walked to the living room and examined the beach and bay below. "This is fantastic. And the pool is beautiful, such a lovely color! I wish I'd brought the grandchildren!"

I rolled my eyes and looked at Shannon.

"I think you'll be happy here. We have provided a cook for you."

"Oh no, we cook our own food—"

"Well then, you will show her how you cook. We have arranged for a couple of catered dinners, and our chef has two helpers who will go to the store for you to get anything you like, within reason. Bear in mind, we don't have a large Indian population, so you might not have all the things you had at home."

"Then I will eat like a person from Florida."

"We call them Floridians."

"Yes, Floridians. I will eat like one of those."

I smiled and had him shown to his bedroom, explaining I had some logistics to attend to.

"Well, that went well," Shannon said as our driver brought us back to our new offices.

"He does this to me every time, always springing things on me. But we're used to it."

Inside the new building, Rhea approached me with a grim look on her face.

"Sorry, Boss, to bring up some bad news. But the Nigerian government is refusing to allow Karin Atkin's plane to land. She was to have an appointment with the Minister of Culture tomorrow morning."

"What's going on?"

"Shall I get Senator Campbell on the line, sir?"

"Please."

Shannon stopped to grab a notebook from her office, checking in with her assistant before following me into my office. I could hear her listening to her messages, but couldn't tell what was being said. Shannon ran to my office alarmed, and we listened to the last message from Paul Vijay together.

"Shannon, Marco has to get the senator involved in this. The control tower is demanding that I land. We are to be escorted by military police and have been notified that the plane will be confiscated. I am not allowed to leave Nigerian airspace without involving their military, and you know what that means."

I was on speaker phone with Senator Campbell.

"What do you mean they've changed their minds, Senator?"

"If you ask me, it's a shakedown. Karin will have funds, right? You usually send her carrying millions."

"She does. But only to pay for advance work, contractors to begin the bidding and ordering process, underground and road crew, and all the planning staff, who, I might add, have already approved this development."

"My guess is they'll take a few million. Your cost of doing business has just gone up."

"But normally, this is negotiated by a State Department rep, someone from the government. I've never been told I'm not allowed to land a plane previously approved for a meeting with a public official without that official making contact. I need more authority than an air traffic controller!"

"Hold on, Senator, you need to listen to this from the pilot, which just came in," I said and played the message.

"Shit," was all Senator Campbell said. "Sounds to me like they've had a coup. I'll have to get with State and find out. And you better get prepared for a rescue mission in case our government gets gutless. You understand?"

"Only too well. Please let me know. I've just greeted the sultan and his wives here in Florida. Got the kids here meeting him. The whole kingdom came, it seems."

"He's probably safer there than in his own palace, Marco. Things are blowing up everywhere."

"Yeah. Have a nice day and get some intel I can rely

on."

I hung up the phone and hit my desk with my fist.

"Dammit! I'm going to have to go over there."

"No. Not yet, Marco. You don't know what you're getting into."

I knew she was scared, but I didn't have much faith in the intelligence gathering from the State Department these days. Policy was more important than truth or accuracy. Success was measured in how not to respond rather than cause confrontations, even if those were going to happen anyway. If we could get into the country, I had assets I could use and even people I could pay to get the information I needed. I knew Karin was in danger. And with all that cash, someone might think this was going to be as good as it gets. Then her usefulness would be devalued.

Her life was on the line.

"I'm the only person to lead this mission, Shannon."

"I'm coming too."

"No, you're not. It's one thing working with me in the office, even working with me on the project there. Even with all your training, it's not enough. This may turn out to be a hostage rescue situation, a full-out combat mission. You have no training in that, sweetheart. Bless you for wanting to help, but now I must get ready to mount this mission. There's a lot at stake."

"Send someone else first. Then you can go."

"Why would I ask someone to risk their life and not risk my own? This is my gig. We don't operate that way, sweetheart."

"But no one would think ill of you sitting this one out. You've just healed from a horrible injury!"

"But you and I know I'm healthy and ready to do it. I couldn't live with myself if I didn't try to save one of my own. They'd do and have done the same for me."

NEARLY TEN HOURS passed until the report came back that the plane had landed and all on board—a small group of six, including Paul—were taken to quarters in a police station outside of the capital, run by one of the warring warlords. Somehow, he was apprised that Karin carried lots of cash, and he didn't want a piece of it.

He wanted all of it.

He didn't need a plane. He already had three others he'd taken in the past week. He was promised troops and equipment from a Russian go-between business-man who had offices in Washington, D.C.

He was on a path he couldn't turn back from now. So he took the money, blew up the plane, and held the hostages, threatening to kill them all if he didn't get a face-to-face meeting with the man who sent the plane.

He wanted a "friendly" sit-down with Marco Gambini.

And I was going to give it to him.

Did you enjoy *Restored*? You won't want to miss the next installment of this wonderful tale of Marco and Shannon in Book 3 of the series, *Revenge*, due out 5/31/22! You can preorder this book here.

authorsharonhamilton.com/portfolio-item/revenge

Are you new to Sharon's books? If you'd like to start at the beginning of all her SEAL stories, try *Accidental SEAL*, which was the book that launched it all! Or read *Ultimate SEAL Collection #1*, which has the first four books in the SEAL Brotherhood series along with two bonus novellas.

Her series order can be found on her website page: Authorsharonhamilton.com.

And so that you never miss a thing, please subscribe to her Newsletter, or follow her on Amazon, BookBub, or GoodReads. All the links are here:

This book, as well as all Sharon's other books, will be coming out in audio, narrated by the Nashville SEAL himself, J.D. Hart. Ordering information can be obtained here.

authorsharonhamilton.com/audiobooks

ABOUT THE AUTHOR

 NYT and USA/Today Bestselling Author Sharon Hamilton's SEAL Brotherhood series have earned her author rankings of #1 in Romantic Suspense, Military Romance and Contemporary Romance. Her other *Brotherhood* stand-alone series are: Bad Boys of SEAL Team 3, Band of Bachelors, True Blue SEALs, Nashville SEALs, Bone Frog Brotherhood, Sunset SEALs, Bone Frog Bachelor Series and SEAL Brotherhood Legacy Series. She is a contributing author to the very popular Shadow SEALs multi-author series.

Her SEALs and former SEALs have invested in two wineries, a lavender farm and a brewery in Sonoma County, which have become part of the new stories. They also have expanded to include Veteran-benefit projects on the Florida Gulf Coast, as well as projects in Africa and the Maldives. One of the SEAL wives has even launched her own women's fiction series. But old characters, as well as children of these SEAL heroes keep returning to all the newer books.

Sharon also writes sexy paranormals in two series: Golden Vampires of Tuscany and The Guardians.

A lifelong organic vegetable and flower gardener, Sharon and her husband lived for fifty years in the Wine Country of Northern California, where many of her stories take place. Recently, they have moved to the beautiful Gulf Coast of Florida, with stories of shipwrecks, the white sugar-sand beaches of Sunset, Treasure Island and Indian Rocks Beaches.

She loves hearing from fans through her website: authorsharonhamilton.com

Find out more about Sharon, her upcoming releases, appearances and news when you sign up for Sharon's newsletter.

Facebook:
facebook.com/SharonHamiltonAuthor

Twitter:
twitter.com/sharonlhamilton

Pinterest:
pinterest.com/AuthorSharonH

Amazon:
amazon.com/Sharon-Hamilton/e/B004FQQMAC

BookBub:
bookbub.com/authors/sharon-hamilton

Youtube:

youtube.com/channel/UCDInkxXFpXp_4Vnq08ZxMBQ

Soundcloud:

soundcloud.com/sharon-hamilton-1

Sharon Hamilton's Rockin' Romance Readers:

facebook.com/groups/sealteamromance

Sharon Hamilton's Goodreads Group:

goodreads.com/group/show/199125-sharon-hamilton-readers-group

Visit Sharon's Online Store:

sharon-hamilton-author.myshopify.com

Join Sharon's Review Teams:

eBook Reviews:

sharonhamiltonassistant@gmail.com

Audio Reviews:

sharonhamiltonassistant@gmail.com

Life is one fool thing after another.

Love is two fool things after each other.

REVIEWS

"An excellent paranormal romance that was exciting, romantic, entertaining and very satisfying to read. It had me anticipating what would happen next many times over, so much so I could not put it down and even finished it up in a day. The vampires in this book were different from your average vampire, but I enjoy different variations and changes to the same old stuff. It made for a more unpredictable read and more adventurous to explore! Vampire lovers, any paranormal readers and even those who love the romance genre will enjoy Honeymoon Bite."

"This is the first non-Seal book of this author's I have read and I loved it. There is a cast-like hierarchy in this vampire community with humans at the very bottom and Golden vampires at the top. Lionel is a dark vampire who are servants of the Goldens. Phoebe is a Golden who has not decided if she will remain human or accept the turning to become a vampire. Either way she and Lionel can never be together since it is forbidden.

I enjoyed this story and I am looking forward to the next installment."

"A hauntingly romantic read. Old love lost and new love found. Family, heart, intrigue and vampires. Grabbed my attention and couldn't put down. Would definitely recommend."

PRAISE FOR THE
SEAL BROTHERHOOD SERIES

"Fans of Navy SEAL romance, I found a new author to feed your addiction. Finely written and loaded delicious with moments, Sharon Hamilton's storytelling satisfies like a thick bar of chocolate." —Marliss Melton, bestselling author of the *Team Twelve* Navy SEALs series

"Sharon Hamilton does an EXCELLENT job of fitting all the characters into a brotherhood of SEALS that may not be real but sure makes you feel that you have entered the circle and security of their world. The stories intertwine with each book before...and each book after and THAT is what makes Sharon Hamilton's SEAL Brotherhood Series so very interesting. You won't want to put down ANY of her books and they will keep you reading into the night when you should be sleeping. Start with this book...and you will not want to stop until you've read the whole series and then...you will be waiting for Sharon to write the next one." (5 Star Review)

"Kyle and Christy explode all over the pages in this first book, *[Accidental SEAL],* in a whole new series of SEALs. If the twist and turns don't get your heart jumping, then maybe the suspense will. This is a must read for those that are looking for love and adventure with a little sloppy love thrown in for good measure." (5 Star Review)

PRAISE FOR THE
BAD BOYS OF SEAL TEAM 3 SERIES

"I love reading this series! Once you start these books, you can hardly put them down. The mix of romance and suspense keeps you turning the pages one right after another! Can't wait until the next book!" (5 Star Review)

"I love all of Sharon's Seal books, but *[SEAL's Code]* may just be her best to date. Danny and Luci's journey is filled with a wonderful insight into the Native American life. It is a love story that will fill you with warmth and contentment. You will enjoy Danny's journey to become a SEAL and his reasons for it. Good job Sharon!" (5 Star Review)

PRAISE FOR THE
BAND OF BACHELORS SERIES

"*[Lucas]* was the first book in the Band of Bachelors series and it was a phenomenal start. I loved how we got to see the other SEALs we all love and we got a look at Lucas and Marcy. They had an instant attraction, and their love was very intense. This book had it all, suspense, steamy romance, humor, everything you want in a riveting, outstanding read. I can't wait to read the next book in this series." (5 Star Review)

PRAISE FOR THE
TRUE BLUE SEALS SERIES

"Keep the tissues box nearby as you read *True Blue SEALs: Zak* by Sharon Hamilton. I imagine more than I wish to that the circumstances surrounding Zak and Amy are all too real for returning military personnel and their families. Ms. Hamilton has put us right in the middle of struggles and successes that these two high school sweethearts endure. I have read several of Sharon Hamilton's military romances but will say this is the most emotionally intense of the ones that I have read. This is a well-written, realistic story with authentic characters that will have you rooting for them and proud of those who serve to keep us safe. This is an author who writes amazing stories that you love and cry with the characters. Fans of Jessica Scott and Marliss Melton will want to add Sharon Hamilton to their list of realistic military romance writers." (5 Star Review)

"Dear FATHER IN HEAVEN,

If I may respectfully say so sometimes you are a strange God. Though you love all mankind,

It seems you have special predilections too.

You seem to love those men who can stand up alone who face impossible odds, Who challenge every bully and every tyrant ~

Those men who know the heat and loneliness of Calvary. Possibly you cherish men of this stamp because you recognize the mark of your only son in them.

Since this unique group of men known as the SEALs know Calvary and suffering, teach them now the mystery of the resurrection ~ that they are indestructible, that they will live forever because of their deep faith in you.

And when they do come to heaven, may I respectfully warn you, Dear Father, they also know how to celebrate. So please be ready for them when they insert under your pearly gates.

Bless them, their devoted Families and their Country on this glorious occasion.

We ask this through the merits of your Son, Christ Jesus the Lord, Amen."

By Reverend E.J. McMalhon S.J. LCDR, CHC, USN
Awards Ceremony SEAL Team One
1975 At NAB, Coronado

Made in the USA
Coppell, TX
20 August 2022

81796782R00138